Outback Roads:
The Nanny

ANNIE SEATON

The Augathella Girls: Book 1

All rights reserved. ISBN 978-0-6452232-2-4

Dedication

This book is dedicated to my loyal readers who love exploring the outback with me.

The Augathella Girls series.

Book 1: Outback Roads –The Nanny

Book 2: Outback Sky – The Pilot

Book 3: Outback Escape – The Sister

Book 4: Outback Winds – The Jillaroo

Book 5: Outback Dawn – The Visitor

Book 6: Outback Moonlight – The Rogue

Book 7: Outback Dust – The Drifter

Book 8: Outback Hope – The Farmer

Augathella Characters

Callie Young	School teacher/ nanny
Braden Cartwright	Owner of *Kilcoy Station*
Rory, Nigel and Petie	Braden's sons
Sophie Cartwright	Braden's sister
Jock Evans	Sophie's partner
Kent Mason	Owner of *Lara Waters*
Kimberley Riordan	School deputy principal
Bob Hamblin	School principal
Jon Ogilvie	Contract cattleman
Jim Anderson	Local garage owner
Jacinta Mason	School teacher
Jen, Nat and Kristie	Callie's best friends

-

Chapter 1

Spring
Brisbane - Friday

As Callie waited for her cue on the raised weather set she glanced over at the news desk. Greg Broadbent, her fiancé and Channel 8 sports broadcaster, had just wound up the sports news for Friday night. With the weekend coming on, and all the associated football codes heading for September finals, Greg's sports report had gone over time—as it often did—and the director's voice had just come through her earbuds telling her she'd lost ninety seconds of her weather segment.

'Speed it up, Calista. None of the pretty sunsets or "have a fabulous weekend" stuff, tonight. Just give 'em the forecast, and cut it short,' Rowan said. She could almost hear his teeth clenching. But Greg was the network's golden-haired boy and he could do what he wanted without penalty.

'Right, got it,' she said.

Damn Greg. As much as she wanted to marry him, his selfish behaviour drove her crazy. She'd wasted an hour preparing her script for the weekend

3

weather wrap-up and trimming it to exactly sixty seconds. The ratings and viewer feedback had proven that her personal touch and comments on the Channel 8 weather segment contributed to the consistently high ratings of the news, sport, and weather hour. Not quite the poster celebrity that Greg was, but her segment was pulling good ratings too.

Greg had been flippant about her careful planning. 'You worry too much, Cal. It's the sport, they want,' he'd said last night. 'And your pretty face and boobs stop the viewers switching channels before the current affairs crew come on. They can look out the window and see the weather for themselves, so it doesn't matter what you say.'

She knew what she should have said to him when he'd dropped his sexist pearl of wisdom, but they'd been in a bar celebrating the ratings improvement with the network guys and Greg had turned his attention away from her to Maxine, the makeup girl, before Callie could protest.

Now thanks to Greg and his blatant disregard for the director, the last minute of the weather would have to be shelved. That was three times in the last month.

'He's a bloody cowboy.' Rowan's voice was short, and it was obvious that Greg was going to cop a serve from the director as soon as they were off air. No matter how many times he was told to

4

wind it up, he'd flash that ten thousand dollar dental-work smile, and go over time.

That dental work meant even though he and Callie were engaged, it was "unofficial" until Greg could afford a ring.

'Forty-five seconds, Calista.'

She took her position on her mark, and stared at the teleprompt where her script waited.

Callie frowned as she scanned quickly through the rainfall and temperature forecast for the greater Brisbane area, and the rest of the Sunshine State for the weekend. Very little sunshine was predicted for the weekend with *la Niña* moving in, but it wasn't the forecast that was making her unsettled tonight. Greg had been strange all week, and she intended having a serious talk to him at dinner tonight. Being Friday, they would go to *his* favourite Italian restaurant at Paddington.

Greg was a stickler for being organised and having a plan. Spontaneity was not in his vocabulary, but Callie was tired of waiting for the plan for an official engagement and wedding date.

It was time to get a firm commitment from Greg; there'd been enough of this "soon" or "at Christmas" for the past two years. Callie's biological clock was ticking louder and faster every day. Jen, Natalie, and Kristie, her three best friends, had seven kids between them already.

Yes, seven!

She wasn't even sporting an engagement ring, and every time she suggested Greg move into her house so he could save the huge rent that he was paying for that luxury riverfront apartment near the Botanic Gardens, he had come up with one excuse or another.

He knew how keen she was to start a family, and her frustration at his "we have plenty of time" attitude was building.

Coffee yesterday with the girls, with only two babies in prams—the rest of the kids were at school or day care—had been a wakeup call, and had added to her discontent.

Her best and long-time friend, Jen, had leaned forward over her soy latte, and picked up Callie's newly manicured hand. 'God, Cal, I'd almost give away one of my kids for a manicure like that. Love that red.' Jen held up her neatly trimmed and unpainted nails. 'I haven't had time for a manicure for three years!'

'Getting married at thirty plus means there's still money for manicures and eating out. Love the matching lipstick too.' Nat's eyes had narrowed as she'd stared at Callie. 'Maybe Calista's the one with the right idea.'

Kristie had shaken her head. 'You're just trying to make her feel better, Nat. I've been wondering how long until we hear a wedding date. I need to lose five kilos.'

'I'm waiting to see the ring that lives up to the manicure,' Jen chipped in.

'Hey, you three.' Callie waved a hand in front of three tired, but happy faces. And yes, she was manicured, but it was for work appearance only. She would happily forgo the hour with Maxine every Monday morning, listening to how drunk the makeup girl had got on the weekend and who she'd slept with. 'I'm still here. And I'm perfectly happy with the way things are.' Despite the lie, she kept her voice upbeat. 'We're unofficially engaged, we just haven't got the ring, or set a date yet. But it won't be long now. And I promise you three will be the first to know.' She turned to Kristie. 'And *you* don't need to lose any weight.'

'Are you, sweets? Happy, I mean?' Jen's voice was low as both Kristie's and Nat's babies started grizzling at the same time. 'And why not? You know my thoughts on Greggie boy. He's not the one for you, trust me.' She shook her head. 'Great teeth, but that's about it.'

Callie had shrugged again. 'It's too late to be looking elsewhere.'

Jen stared at her. 'See? I rest my case. If you really loved him, you wouldn't even think of saying that.'

'No, you misunderstood me.'

'Did I?' Jen had always been shrewd.

'Calista!'

Callie jumped and brought her thoughts back to the weather program as the director's voice filled her ears.

'For God's sake, Calista. Stop daydreaming, ten seconds and you're on. Camera one. Jack, ready to swing in. Sweep from Greg after the ad. Boyd, be ready to switch to the synoptics charts when Callie is thirty seconds in.'

Callie straightened and looked over to the news desk where the set lights reflected on Greg's perfectly coiffured hair. Yep, Jen was right,. It was time.

Tonight was the night. They would set a firm date for the wedding.

I can wait for an engagement ring.

##

'So a wet weekend,' Callie finished up four minutes later. ''Stay dry, folks and have a great weekend. See you on—'

Her words were interrupted by Rowan swearing loudly and static in her ear buds. 'What the friggin' hell is he bloody doing now?'

Callie looked across to the monitor behind the floor manager. Both cameras had panned to Greg who was kneeling in front of Maxine. Maxine, their make-up artist.

Greg. Callie's mouth dropped open as he opened a ring box and held up a huge sparkling diamond in front of Maxine.

Suddenly the sound switched from her back to the news desk and Callie drew a sharp breath.

'Maxine, my love. Will you marry me?' Greg took her hand.

'Oh, sweet cheeks,' Maxine purred in her annoying little girl voice. 'Of course I will.'

For a few seconds shock held Callie rigid. Then without thinking, and paying no attention to the cameras, she stepped down off the weather set and strode across to the news desk.

Rowan's voice was gleeful in her earbud. 'Follow her, cameras two and three. Oh, ratings heaven, guys.'

'You lowlife, double-timing piece of shit. What the hell are you playing at, *sweet cheeks*?' Pushing between Greg and Maxine, Callie shoved at his shoulder with one beautifully manicured red fingernail and was not one bit remorseful when he overbalanced and fell onto his Armani-clad backside.

'You've hurt him,' Maxine squealed and dropped to the floor beside Greg—who looked ridiculous—as Callie turned away fighting a mix of tears and temper, just as both cameras zoomed in for a closeup. Of *her* face.

Chapter 2

Kilcoy Station - Sunday

Braden Cartwright tilted his head to the side listening as he sat at his desk entering the day's cattle weights into the spreadsheet. He could have sworn he'd heard a car door shut, but he hadn't heard a vehicle come into the house yard. He turned back to the computer and then jumped when the back screen door slammed.

'You there, Bray?'

He stood and stretched before he made his way down the hall to the kitchen.

As he closed the study door behind him, he frowned as his boys' excited voices came from outside.

'Soph, what's happening? I wasn't expecting you guys this weekend.' He rubbed a hand over his unshaven face as he walked into the kitchen. 'Have I stuffed up the dates again?'

His sister was standing at the fridge unloading an esky full of food onto the empty shelves.

'What's wrong? What are you doing?' he asked as she kept her back to him.

11

'No. You didn't stuff up the dates. I'm filling your fridge because I knew there'd be nothing here. What the hell do you live on, Braden?'

'I was going to the pub for a steak in a while.'

'Before or after you drank the six pack that's in here?' Sophie's back was ramrod straight and her movements were jerky. 'And then you were going to drive forty ks home in the dark after more beer and a steak?'

'Yes, I was. What's wrong with that? I have to eat. What's going on? Is everything all right? Are the boys okay?'

'Yes, your boys are fine.'

'So what's happening? Is Jock with you?'

Sophie closed the fridge door and turned to him. Her eyes were ringed with dark mauve shadows and her usually smiling lips were set in a straight line. 'What's happening is that it's time for some tough love. There's no easy way for me to do this, and it's caused me a lot of sleepless nights.'

'Do what?'

'I've brought the boys home because Jock and I are moving to Innot Springs.'

'What?' Braden stared at her.

'Jock's giving up the helicopter mustering. He's been offered a job managing a property.'

'Where the hell is Innot Springs? I've never heard of it.'

'On the Atherton Tablelands.'

'What! That's too far to take the boys away.'

'Yes, you're damn right it is. It's eleven hundred kilometres north and that's why they're here now. They've come home. Almost two years away from their father and their real home is too long. I've given you as much time as I could, Bray, but it's time for you to take responsibility before Rory, Nigel, and Petie think that Jock and I are their parents. Petie's starting to call me Mummy. It's way past time that they came home to you.'

'Now hang on, Soph.' Shock rippled through Braden. He'd never seen his sister like this before. She was usually full of joy; this angry person was not his giggly little sister.

Although not so little any more. He was thirty-one, so that made her twenty-three.

'No. *You* hang on. I know what you've been through and I—we, Jock too—have gone above and beyond for you. This is the only way to do it. If we stayed at Augathella, you'd talk me around and the boys would stay with us. Jock and I have our own lives, and he's given me an ultimatum. It's him or the boys.' Her voice shook. 'I'm only twenty-three years old, Bray, and I can't do it anymore. I spent my twenty-first birthday changing Petie's nappies.'

Braden ran his hand through his hair as disbelief took hold. 'Look, I—'

'No! You listen to me for a change. I'm not budging, no matter what you say. It's two years since Julia left us.' Sophie's voice shook. 'Yes, she left *all* of us. Not just you. The boys and me too. And we are slowly learning to live with it. You can't wallow here by yourself forever, Braden. Working yourself to death, living on beer and pub food.' She came over and held his arm, her work-roughened fingers pressing hard into his skin. 'You have three sons out there and it's time to start being a father again to those beautiful little boys. I can't do it anymore.'

'When?' he managed to choke out. 'When are you moving?'

'Now. The removalists are coming for our furniture tomorrow. Jock'll be over in a while to pick me up. Kent's getting a new pilot for the next muster.'

Before Braden could speak, the back door opened and three small bodies tumbled in, followed by three puppies.

'We're hungry, Aunty Soph. Hi, Dad. Look at our new puppies.' Rory, his eldest at eight, lifted an ugly brindle pup and put it against his face. 'This is Bumper.'

'And mine's called Tweedle, Dad.' Nigel held one of the other pups up high. He squealed as a stream of wee trickled down his arm. 'You little bugger!'

'Nigel. Language.' Sophie held Braden's eyes steadily as Petie, the youngest at almost four, walked across to her and clung to her leg.

Braden crouched down and kept his voice even. 'Who's got a hug for Daddy?'

Rory and Nigel raced into his open arms, but Petie held back.

'Good to see you, fellas,' he said as both boys planted a sloppy kiss on his unshaven cheek.

'We're coming home to live with you, Dad. I can help you with the cattle. Nige and I are so excited.' Rory's voice was full of self-importance. 'But Petie's being a sook. But don't worry we'll look after him when you haven't got time.'

Braden nodded and swallowed back the emotion as he held his sister's eyes. Eyes that were awash with tears as she nodded.

'Yes, you are coming home.' He moved away from the boys and reached out to Petie as Sophie gave his youngest a gentle push in Braden's direction. 'Rory and Nigel, you go and get your stuff out of Aunty Sophie's car and then you can choose what rooms you want. We live in this side of the house now. When you choose, I'll move your stuff over.' He swung Petie up into his arms, and his eyes stung with tears as he buried his face in the hair that smelled of the baby shampoo Julia had

15

used on the other two when they were little. 'Now tell me, my little man. Do you have a puppy too?'

'I do.' Petie's voice was as gravelly as ever.

'What's his name?'

'*Her* name is Apricot.'

Braden hid the smile that tugged at his mouth. 'Apricot, hmm.' He met Sophie's eyes over the top of Petie's head. She nodded again and wiped the back of her hand over her eyes.

As the boys lugged their stuff in from the boot of the Camry station wagon, Sophie helped Braden make up their beds in the room they chose.

'We've been calling her Cottie,' Sophie said. 'Easier to call her in from the yard.'

'Dad, Nigel locked the toilet door on his way out and I'm busting,' Rory yelled down the hall.

'Use the one in the laundry.'

'Petie's in there doing a poo,' Nigel called from the bathroom.

'Go out on the grass then. But just this once, Rory. Nigel, you get a screwdriver and unlock that door.' Braden rolled his eyes as Sophie's grin appeared for the first time. 'I can't get you to change your mind, can I, sis?'

'Nope. You'd better get used to it, Bray. Petie still needs a hand wiping his bum. You go and help him and I'll finish making the beds.'

Braden took off down the hall, tripped over a puppy outside the laundry and then slipped in a wet patch outside the open toilet door.

'Apricot had an accident, Daddy. But I'm *such* a good boy. I can get on the big toilet by myself now.' Petie's blue eyes—so like Julia's—were wide. 'And I can wipe my own bottom too.'

'You *are* a good boy.' Braden quickly dealt with Petie's needs and lifted him down. 'Go and wash your hands. I'll be right behind you.' Braden shook his head as he followed Petie to the bathroom. He was still shellshocked and took little notice of the mud on the floor. As he supervised the handwashing and scrubbed his own hands, a bloodcurdling yell came from the kitchen. He and Sophie arrived in the doorway at the same time. Nigel sat astride Rory, pummelling his brother's chests with his fists.

'You're a dobber.'

'Get off your brother and go and sort out that locked toilet door right now, Nigel Cartwright.' Braden reached down and grabbed Nigel by the scruff of his shirt, and tried to hold his temper in.

Nigel took off up the hall, muttering under his breath.

'You'll have to watch his language, Braden, I don't know where he's picking it up, but he's had a cake of soap in his mouth a couple of times lately.'

17

Sophie crossed to the esky and put the lid back on it. 'There's Jock now. We're going to leave my car here and take the Land Cruiser. I thought if you take my suggestions on board, you could do with a station wagon. She's a bit old but good enough to get into town, and there's a booster seat in the back for Petie.'

'Suggestions?' he asked cautiously. What suggestions? Did I miss something?'

'No. We didn't get a chance to talk. I have a list of sites here for you to get on and look for a nanny. And some other staff. With the insurance'—her voice wobbled again—'I know you can afford it, Bray. You need help here. You can't do it by yourself. I'm sorry we're moving away. I really am.'

He nodded slowly. 'Thank you. I'll look at it after the boys go to bed.'

Sophie held her arms out and when Braden held her she put her head on his shoulder. 'I'm sorry, it was a very hard choice to make. I'm going to miss you and the boys so much. Even though you're a cranky pants, remember I do love my big brother.'

'I know, sis. And I love you. I owe you the world for what you've done.' Braden leaned back and held Sophie's shoulders gently as he looked down at her. 'And don't worry. You're right. It's time. Now that the shock's passed, I'll be fine. We'll cope. I want you to be happy too.'

He waited a moment as he looked closely at her. 'Are you sure you want to move so far away?'

Her reply came slowly. 'It's where Jock wants to be. So, I guess if I love Jock, I'll be going.'

Chapter 3

Fortitude Valley, Brisbane - Tuesday

'And your experience with children, Ms Young?' The woman behind the desk scanned the resumé Callie had put together over the weekend after she'd searched Jobs Online and emailed to the agency yesterday afternoon. She'd been stunned to get a call first thing this morning inviting her to interview. The response had been much quicker than she'd expected.

'I see you have a primary teaching qualification. Were you ever employed by a school?'

'Yes, I worked at Barfield State School for three years after I graduated.' Callie reached down into her bag and pulled out the folder with the original references inside. 'These are references from the principal, the deputy principal, and my supervising teacher.'

The woman nodded and took them; there was silence as she read through them.

'And why did you leave? It looks like you were highly regarded.'

'I was offered a job with a television network that I thought was better hours and pay, and that I'd enjoy.' Callie stared at the clock on the wall.

'And now you want to go back to working with children?'

Callie nodded. 'Yes.'

I should never have left teaching, she thought.

But Greg had been persuasive and told her that it would mean them having holidays at the same time, and a better salary, once she worked her way up at the television station. He'd hated that she had more holidays than his four weeks a year.

She'd met Greg at a riverside bar near Queen Street one Friday night a few months after her parents had died, and her grief had left her confidence at a low ebb. He'd asked her out and they were soon a couple. At the time she had deferred to Greg to make the decisions, and when he suggested she leave teaching and take a job that he'd wangled for her at Channel 8, Callie had foolishly listened to him. Over the three and a bit years they'd been together, they'd been to heaps of weddings, including those of her best friends, and watched them settle into homes and start their families.

That was all Callie had ever wanted. Her parents were both gone, and she'd been an only child and she'd yearned to be married and raise a family in her beautiful house. Three kids was her plan, but she could never engage Greg in a conversation about a timeline for their future or how many kids he wanted. He was more interested in talking about their financial future and always dragging her off to investment advisers to invest her money.

Her money.

'Plenty of time, Calista. No need to rush. We need to get our investments in place.'

But there wasn't plenty of time and she'd wasted three years of her life with that lowlife. Thank goodness she'd not given into any of the schemes he and the financial adviser had come up with. In hindsight that was when he'd started to pull back a bit.

Jen had been right all along, and Callie knew she'd been naive. She'd dreamed of her happy family in the future, and if she was totally honest, Greg had never been a part of the image in her head.

Now the only image she had of him was him on his knees proposing to Maxine on television.

Her stomach churned and Callie bit down on her lip, pushing away the nausea that threatened. She felt like such a gullible fool.

Rowan had called her into his office when she'd put in her notice yesterday and said, 'Calista, the ratings have gone through the roof. You're a star. The CEO has refused to accept your resignation. He's offered you a pay rise.'

'No. And please don't call me Calista. You know I prefer Callie.'

Rowan's eyes narrowed and his voice was cunning. 'More than Greg's salary. A lot more.' He sat back and folded his arms.

'He humiliated me.' Callie's hands clenched on her lap. 'And I totally humiliated myself. And in front of most of Queensland. I'm sorry, Rowan, but I'm out of here. I'm not going on air again.'

Rowan's assistant, Julia, had tapped on the door. 'Callie, you're trending on Insta and the vid has gone viral on Tik Tok. It's got over a million views already. International too. You're famous. You're hash tagged *#wrong forecast*.'

'Name your price, Calis—Callie, and I'm sure the CEO will meet it.' Rowan smiled at her.

'No way. If you think I can front the public ever again or work with *him*, you are kidding yourselves.' She'd almost spat the words as she looked through the glass door of Rowan's office and watched Greg cosying up to Maxine. The bitch had put on an Oscar-worthy performance on Friday night when the camera was on her, but had stopped crying as soon as Rowan had called cut, and the seven o'clock current affairs show broadcast from the next studio, filled the screen.

23

'Whatever they've offered we'll top,' Rowan stated. 'And give you a sports car, and maybe look at finding you an apartment on the river.'

How ironic.

'I have a sports car and I already have a perfectly suitable house on the river, thank you.' Rowan didn't know she was very comfortable financially, and he probably didn't need to, but his smug expression changed to surprise.

'Anyway, they?' Callie had frowned. 'Who's they?'

Julia pointed to Callie's desk. 'You've had calls from most of the major networks in the country.'

'No. No chance at all.' She turned to Rowan. 'Just get them to make up my pay, and take off whatever notice I had to give.'

'Who's going to do the weather segment tonight? You'll lose your standing in the entertainment industry, Callie.'

'Maybe Maxine could,' Callie had said sweetly as she'd headed to her office to pack up the few personal items she had in there.

'Ms Young?'

Callie lifted her head and stared at the agency woman across the desk who was holding her references out to her. 'Sorry, what did you say?'

'I said, you have excellent references. If you are happy to wait here, I just have to make a call and I can give you a decision.'

'What, today?'

'Yes. But I have one more question, and then I'll be honest with you. I'd hate you to change your mind if you do decide to take the position.'

'Yes? What's the question?'

'We interviewed all day yesterday, and we didn't have a single person interested in the position, so I'd rather be up front with you before I call the employer.'

'What's the problem with the job?'

'The isolation. It's a large cattle station in remote outback Queensland, with the closest major towns four hundred kilometres away. No shops, no restaurants or clubs, no cinema. Is that a problem for you?'

Callie smiled and shook her head. 'Not one bit. The more remote the better. But I do have one question for you. Is there television reception out there?'

The agency woman frowned. 'I really don't know, but I can ask for you when I make the call.' She stared at Callie for a moment. 'I thought you looked familiar. Didn't you work at Channel 8?' Callie's stomach sank as the woman's face broke into a grin. 'I know! You're the Tik Tok weather girl. Why on earth do you want to go to the outback?''

'I've decided to go back to teaching.' She leaned forward and spoke firmly. 'The further away from Brisbane the better.'

The woman closed her mouth and left Callie in the office.

Chapter 4

Kilcoy Station - Tuesday

By noon on Tuesday, Braden was exhausted. It wasn't that the boys had been naughty or extra demanding, but the number of things he had to keep in his head were wearing him out.

Had they all had enough decent food to eat?

Had Petie been to the loo by himself? Note to self, check his underdaks.

Had Nigel and Rory done the schoolwork he'd given them after morning tea? It was awfully quiet in the schoolroom on the veranda behind the living room where they were doing the morning's school work. Sophie had organised Distance Education from Brisbane for them, until Braden could chase up school of the air. She'd driven them to the small state school at Augathella from their place and Petie had gone to kindy two days a week, but it was too far from *Kilcoy Station* for Braden to take them into town every day.

Ring School of the Air.

Another job to add to the growing list.

Don't forget to send the online grocery order.

Don't forget to pick it up.

27

Feed the dogs and put them outside for a toilet break.

Remember to bring the dogs in. He'd seen a few snakes on the move last week.

Warn the boys about not leaving the house yard.

Don't forget to call Sophie at eight tonight to tell her everything is okay.

It wasn't okay, because the agency hadn't had any luck finding a nanny so far, but he wouldn't worry her.

He also wanted to have a chat about Jock, and make sure she was doing the right thing, moving away with him. Braden knew he owed his sister big time. Sophie was right; maybe he'd wallowed for too long and given up responsibility for his boys too easily, but Julia leaving them so suddenly had left him unable to function for the first couple of months.

Okay, maybe he was weak, but losing Julia had been a huge shock and had shattered him; since he'd stopped taking the sleeping pills two years ago he still had nightmares most nights.

Don't go there. No point.

Afterwards Sophie had stepped in and offered to take the boys for a while, until Braden got himself sorted. To be honest, he found it hard to even look at them, because blue-eyed Rory and Petie looked so much like their mother. He had put the little energy he had left into the cattle station, and the months had raced by. Then a year, then two years. Every time Sophie had brought the boys over to see him, it got a little bit easier, but—

Braden lifted his head and listened. The house was way too quiet. When he'd come in earlier, he'd heard Rory and Nigel talking, but now there was an ominous quiet.

Damn it to hell, what were they doing?'

He pushed the chair back and hurried down to the schoolroom. It was empty. With a frown he walked quickly down the hall to the TV room where he'd left Petie watching cartoons. That room was empty too and the television was off.

Shit, where are they? His temper eased as a tendril of worry pushed its way up into his throat and he swallowed.

I can't do this.

You have to.

'Rory! Nigel! Where are you? Petie!' Braden bellowed as he pounded down the hall. He pushed open the kitchen door and stopped dead. Three innocent—and vegemite-covered—faces stared at him.

'What are you doing in here?'

Petie's bottom lip quivered.

'Petie was hungry.' Rory put his arm around his little brother and nodded at Braden. 'You were

29

busy, Dad, and it was lunchtime so I made sandwiches for us. Do you want one? Aunty Soph taught me how to make vegemite or peanut butter sandwiches because I can use the butter knife to make them. I'm not allowed to use a sharp knife, although I reckon I could now that we're home. What do you think?'

Guilt stormed through Braden. He walked over to the table, gently touched Petie's shoulder and crouched down beside Rory.

'Mate, you're a champion. Thanks for making sandwiches for your brothers. And yes, I'd love you to make a peanut butter one for me, but you probably don't know—because Aunty Soph always told me it was gross—that I have strawberry jam with my peanut butter too.'

'Ew, that's gross, Dad. You won't catch me eating it, but I'll give it a go for you.'

'I want jam too, like Daddy,' Petie piped up, his little face clearing into a wide smile.

An ache formed behind Braden's eyes, and his chest tightened; as he stood there he vowed he would do the best he could for his three boys.

They were good kids, and they deserved more from him. It was way overdue. He had to get his head together and focus on them. They were his number one priority.

'Guys, I—' He jumped as the house phone rang. 'I'll just get that and then I'll make chocolate milkshakes. Don't go away.'

He hurried back to the study and picked up the phone. '*Kilcoy Station*, Braden Cartwright speaking.'

'Oh Mr Cartwright, I was hoping you'd be there. It's Siobhan McPherson from Jobs Online. I have an extremely suitable candidate for you.'

'Great. When can she—he—start?'

'We haven't discussed that yet. It's really up to you to decide if she is suitable. Callie was a primary school teacher, and she presents as a very sensible and competent young woman. I can email the application and references now that we've completed the interview.'

'Ms McPherson, if you're happy, I'm satisfied. I'm sure you've had much more experience in filling jobs that I ever have. Just tell me what I need to do.'

'Ah, before that, there is one question she wanted me to ask you. Do you have television reception out there?'

Braden rolled his eyes. God, no one wanted to come this far out, and as soon as there was a suitable person, she was going to knock it back because she couldn't watch the soapies. He cleared his throat. 'In good weather, tell her we can pick up

Imparja from the Territory, but there's no other free to air TV, I'm sorry. We have a DVD player and internet access *most* of the time. Via satellite.' He knew his words were tumbling over each other, but he was desperate to get someone out here as soon as the agency could send someone. 'Oh and Netflix, of course, when the internet reception is good.'

'Okay, I'll let her know. I won't be a moment. Please hold the line.'

As Braden waited, he could hear murmured voices. It was only a moment before Ms McPherson came back on.

'Ms Young has accepted the position. We just have to complete the paperwork and I'll email it to you. Once you approve it, I'll give her your contact number and she can call you directly with any questions. I told her there is some urgency and she's happy to head out to Augathella tomorrow.'

'Where does she live?

'Brisbane.'

'I'll organise a flight for her. That'll be quicker.'

'Just a moment.'

Braden waited again as the muffled voices sounded in the background.

'No, she wants to drive. She has her own car, and prefers to bring it with her.'

'Tell her . . . wait . . . can I please talk to her now? I'll sign the paperwork and get it back to you, and it'll save time if we can make the plans now. Ms McPherson, I'm desperate.'

'I can't see a problem. I'll email you the papers now while you speak to her. Here she is. This is Callie Young.'

Braden waited until a tentative voice spoke. 'Hello?'

'Hello, Ms Young. I'm Braden Cartwright. Thanks for speaking to me, and thanks for agreeing to work out here. I'm really pleased that you've accepted.'

'I'm grateful for the opportunity, Mr Cartwright.'

'I'd like to get you out here as soon as we can. I have a mate I can organise to pick you up at Archerfield Airport and bring you direct to *Kilcoy Station*. Can you come tomorrow?'

'I can, but I am going to drive out.'

'There's no need. There's a car here for you to use. A station wagon.'

He widened his eyes when she spoke firmly.

'I will *not* be told what to do, Mr Cartwright. I'll drive myself out to Augathella. When you send the forms back to Siobhan, please also attach directions. And please email me if there's anything else that I'll need out there. If I need to bring anything.'

'You do know how far it is, don't you?'

Her reply was a while coming. 'Yes, I do, but I prefer to drive.'

'Okay, I'll expect you about Friday or Saturday then.'

'Ah, okay. I'll see you then.'

Braden hung up, downloaded his email and signed the forms without looking at them, and sent them straight back. Now he had four days to spend in the house with the boys.

They'd make the most of it. He could see what Rory and Nigel were up to with their schoolwork. He could afford to take four days off the property—until the nanny arrived. He'd get a couple of extra stockmen sent over for the rest of the week. There was a mob to be moved in before the big muster, but it could be done on horseback.

He picked up the phone to leave a message for Kent Mason, his mate, and the station manager at *Lara Waters*, the neighbouring property. Braden's head stockman, Jim had gone over there with the cattle truck this morning.

Kent picked up straight away.

'Hey, Kent. Just a quick one, mate. When Jim arrives with the truck, can you let him know I'll be caught up for the rest of the week. Ask him to organise a couple of extra blokes to come back over with him for a few days, on his way back through town this afternoon.'

'Will do. Everything okay there?'

Braden nodded silently as noise carried down the hall. The sound of his boys' giggles lightened his heart and he couldn't help smiling.

'Yeah, mate. Actually very okay. My boys have come home.'

'Great news, Braden. It'll be good to see them. It's been a while.'

'How about you? A bit of a shock that Jock's moving.'

'Yeah, he mentioned something vague the other day, but I didn't realise they were moving away until he finished up yesterday. Muster pilots are in short supply as always. If you hear of anyone around the traps, let me know.'

'Mate, the only traps I'll be in the next few weeks is in the house. Cooking and looking after the boys.'

'True. I'll come over for a beer one night. You'll miss Soph.'

'I will. But we'll get used to it. And I'll hold you to that beer.'

'Great, I'll look forward to it.'

Braden was thoughtful as he hung up the phone. Kent and Sophie had gone out at high school and they'd been tight for a couple of years afterwards. Braden had been disappointed when they'd broken up; Kent would have made a great brother-in-law. He'd never thought much of Jock but it wasn't up to him to pick his sister's partner. Life was so uncertain, you had to go for what you wanted.

When you wanted it, he thought.

Braden shook his head as he headed for the kitchen to make the three promised milkshakes.

Stuff it. He'd make four. There'd be no beer drinking here while he was looking after his boys.

Chapter 5

Brisbane - Tuesday 5.30 p.m.

'Jen, I need a favour. Are you free for a couple of hours?' Callie said when Jen answered the call.

'I am. Damien's just home from work, and both the kids are bathed and ready for bed. I was going to call you and ask you out for a wine tonight anyway.'

'Maybe after.'

'Are you okay, love?'

'Never been better.' Callie stood on the wide front veranda and watched a couple of honeyeaters drinking nectar from the blooms hanging over the fence. The garden was a riot of colour and she was so going to miss her home. She swallowed. 'I need you as soon as you can get away to keep a look out for me.'

'Huh? A look out? What are you up to?'

'I'm retrieving *my* car. The one *I* paid for.'

'The Mazda Roadster? You go, girl. That will tick Greg off big time.'

'That's the one. And a few other things too. And Jen, I have lots to tell you. I'll wait in the foyer while you knock on the door.'

'Are you really okay, Cal?'

37

'I am. I'm doing what I should have done two years ago. Meet me at the entrance to the gardens. I'll grab a City Cat.'

'Okay, I'll be there within the hour.'

Callie walked down to the river and waited at the Milton ferry terminal. It didn't take long to travel the four stops and walk to the gate of the gardens. Jen was already there waiting for her.

'Thanks, Jen. Did you have any trouble getting a park?'

Jen gave her a quick hug. 'Damien heard me say we were going for a wine and he dropped me in. I'll get a taxi home.' She stepped back and looked at Callie. 'So what's the plan?'

'I have to get into the apartment block to get down to the basement garage, and that won't be a problem. Greg's at work, but I want to be sure Maxine's not there. There's a couple of things I need to get—'

'As well as the sports car?' Jen asked drily. 'The one he called "*our* car" and wouldn't let you keep at your place, even though *you* paid for it.'

'That's the one. *My* car. And all the other things I paid for over the three years, and some of Nan's good china that he took a liking to.'

'You go, girl! I know that TikTok garbage must be hard, but it'll be a flash in the pan. When do you go back to work?'

'I don't. I quit. And I'm going back teaching. I've got a job already.'

'Wow, that's excellent. Which school?'

Callie pulled a face. 'Ah, not in Brissie.'

'Up the coast?'

She shook her head. 'No. I've taken on a nannying position at Augathella. Or rather on a property out that way.'

'What! Augathella? Isn't that way out in the outback?' Jen's mouth dropped open. 'That's the last place I'd expect you to go. You're such a city girl, Cal. What about your lovely house?'

'Sure is "way out in the outback". New horizons and all that. Plus there's no TV reception out there, so the family I'm going to help out will be part of the tiny handful of people in the whole world who didn't witness my humiliation.'

'It wasn't humiliation. It was giving Greg what he deserved. Good riddance to him, and a lovely public one.'

'It's still a bit raw, and a bit embarrassing. I'm going to lie low for a while where no one knows me. You've got no idea how many people have laughed at me. Even the woman who interviewed me at the agency had seen it.'

'It wasn't *at* you, Callie. It was with you, and how you showed that jerk up.' Jen laughed. 'Or should I say pushed him down? You were superb.

And don't you worry; slimy, sleazy Greg came across exactly as he is and so did that skank.'

'Oh, God. Did you see it live too?' Callie rolled her eyes.

'I did. You were on fire. Must have been great for the ratings.'

'Apparently.'

'I was waiting for them to put a soundtrack on it. You know that Helen Reddy song. Would have made a perfect theme. You were *invincible*.'

'I still get all prickly hot when I think about it. And then I get so angry at Greg.'

'Hold that anger, sweetheart. There's no need for you to take off. It'll blow over. What are you going to do with your house if you go?'

'*When* I go. Lock it up and leave it empty. It'll be there when I decide to come back to the city.'

'As long as you do.'

'I will. And I'll get a job in another school in a year or two. When I'm not the famous *#wrongforecast* weather girl.'

Jen glanced at her as they walked to Eagle Street where Greg's apartment was on the second top floor.

'I can see where you're coming from, but I'll miss you. Tell me a bit about this job you're going to.'

'It's a nannying job. Some teaching too, I guess.'

'You guess? Have you got a statement of duties?'

'Not yet.'

'And what about the family. Are they decent? Have they got references?'

Callie chuckled. 'I was the one who had to have references.'

'Well, do you know anything about them?'

'Not a lot,' she admitted.

Jen put her hands on her hips. 'Honestly, Cal, you are so trusting. You're going to the outback!'

'And that means what?'

'You've seen the movies. *Wolf Creek, Razorback*, and then there's all those people who go missing out there. That new series on STAN. What was it called?'

'*The Tourist*.' Callie rolled her eyes. 'But you're exaggerating.'

'No, you're trusting too easily again. I might be mean, but think of Greg and how you trusted him. He's stuffed up your life and your career. And one of my friend's sisters went out to a nanny job, and she was expected to look after the kids, the house, the cooking and the washing and ironing. Apparently the wife did nothing but sit around all day and play at being lady of the house.'

'Did she leave?'

Jen grinned. 'Um no. It sort of worked out. She ended up being wife number two.'

'You're making that up.' Callie nudged Jen with her elbow as they approached the luxury apartment block.

'Okay, maybe a little bit. But she did end up with the farmer. So where do you want me?' Jen asked.

'I called the station and asked to speak to Maxine, to make sure she was there, but they said she's on leave. I want you to knock on the door and make sure she's not in the apartment, and then, if the coast's clear, I'll go and get my things while you keep watch.'

'Is there much?'

'Just my Nan's Wedgewood dinner set, and a couple of pieces of Venetian glass that Greg took a fancy to. Three trips down to the car max.'

Jen shook her head. 'Lowlife. I was right, wasn't I? I can think of worse names too.'

Callie sighed. 'You were. And don't you worry, I've called him a lot of things over the weekend.' She pulled out the key to the apartment as they approached the foyer on the river side. 'Ready?'

'Yep. Let's do this, and then we'll go have a drink. Damien said he'll put the kids to bed.'

'Thanks, Jen. You're a good friend. And you're lucky. Damien is a great guy.'

Jen nodded. 'He is. And I'm a friend you'll learn to listen to next time when I tell you *your* guy is a jerk of the first order.'

'There's not going to be a next time!'

Jen waited as Callie inserted the key. 'I'll ring you when it's all clear.' She chuckled as the door opened and they stepped into the foyer. 'I just wish I could see Greg's face when he discovers you've taken *your* car.'

Chapter 6

The Warrego Highway - Thursday 9.30am

Doubts niggled at Callie a couple of times on the first day of driving west in her red sports car. Maybe it had been a bit of a knee jerk reaction, and her decision to go so far away from Brisbane—where she'd always lived—might have been a bit over the top. It had been hard pulling the door shut on her house, and the little honeyeater had looked at her balefully as if he too wondered what the hell she was doing.

'Me too, little bird,' she'd said wistfully. 'The only thing I know about the outback is what I've seen in the movies.'

Her doubts as to whether she'd made the right call vanished when she stopped at Toowoomba for her first coffee and the girl in the coffee shop had recognised her and asked for her autograph.

Her bloody autograph!

So I did the make the right decision, and I'll stop worrying.

With no family to worry about and having once led an independent life—before Greg—told her she could do this.

'I can,' she told herself over and over again as her little red sports car chewed up the kilometres. 'I will do it.'

Braden Cartwright had attached the directions as promised and when Callie had printed them out at home, and pulled up Google Maps on her laptop her heart almost stopped beating. No wonder he'd offered to fly her out there. It was such a long way.

She didn't know anything about the job, the place, the children or the setup out there. When Jen had asked for details and Callie couldn't give her any, Jen had frowned.

'Do you know what you're heading for?'

'Not exactly, but it's a bona fide agency, so there's nothing to worry about.'

'You ring me as soon as you get out there. If you have any doubt, turn around and come straight home.'

'Yes, I promise.' She'd pulled a face at Jen, but appreciated her best friend's concern and took it on board. Maybe she *should* have got more details.

Glancing down at the sat nav on the dashboard, she calculated how long it was before she would take her next break.

A long time between towns.

Hmmm.

45

Chapter 7

Chinchilla - Thursday afternoon

Eight hundred and thirty kilometres of driving, Google Maps told Callie as she peered at her phone screen. When she'd set off, she'd followed the instructions about which road to take and where to stop for fuel and coffee, although she thought Braden Cartwright had been a bit presumptuous telling her where to stop the first night. And not only telling her where to stop, he'd *also* booked and paid for the motel room. Callie was tempted to ignore it and find her own accommodation. She woke up to herself in time and realised she was letting Greg's behaviour dictate her reactions to a person who was simply trying to ease her way out to her new job.

It had been very kind of her new employer to map out a route, and book and pay for the accommodation, although by the time she'd swung her car into the highway motel car park, her back and legs were aching from being in the car so long. She could feel how far she'd driven that day.

After Toowoomba when she left cityscapes behind, the landscape had turned to yellow and gold. Flat paddocks and straight roads, passing the occasional road train—the first Callie had ever seen—had made for a pretty drive that had gone very quickly as she'd focused on her driving. On the second day of driving, the morning mist had lifted by the time Callie reached the little town her new employer recommended for a break.

The old fashioned grocery store had a coffee shop at the front and she ordered coffee and cake to take away. When the woman handed her the coffee without any recognition or any smart "TikTok girl" comments, Callie relaxed and sat outside feeling quite anonymous. It was a beautiful clear day, so before she headed west again, she put down the soft top of her roadster.

The drive to Chinchilla was uneventful but she was tired by the time she pulled up for the night. As she locked the car door and headed for the reception office of the Highway Motel, she nodded.

Good job, Callie, she muttered. No one need know it was the longest distance she'd ever driven. Once she was out on this outback station, seemingly far flung and not close to any town according to the map, she'd have to be careful not to show her lack of country awareness and experience.

Not to mention knowledge. Callie had lived in Brisbane her entire life. Apart from two flights to Sydney to visit her Great Aunt Pattie—her only living relative—and then one memorable trip to the

47

resort on Pentecost Island in the Whitsundays with Greg, she had never left Brisbane.

She frowned as she thought of the trip to Pentecost Island and blocked the memory.

Decidedly unpleasant. The resort and the staff had been wonderful but Greg's behaviour had been appalling. She'd considered breaking up with him then, but had stupidly let him talk her around.

'I'm stressed, love. When I'm away from the studio, my confidence goes and I'm scared they'll replace me,' he'd said.

Refusing to think of anything more to do with Greg and blocking the image of his proposal to his new woman from her thoughts, Callie dragged her overnight bag from the back seat and headed to the office.

The bell above the reception office door tinkled as she pushed it open and stepped into the icy air-conditioned foyer. Even though it was only September, it was hotter than she was used to at this time of the year, and Callie appreciated the cooler air as she stepped inside.

After five minutes of ringing the bell on the desk, and shivering in the cool air, Callie contemplated going back to her car, and continuing her journey; there were still a couple of hours before dark. A brief thought popped in unbidden; maybe she could just keep going and make this a road trip? Maybe she could ring Mr Cartwright and tell him she'd changed her mind. She could keep driving and go to any of the destinations on his map, and then keep just heading off into the wilds, maybe even to the Northern Territory.

No one would know her there, surely. Hopefully they didn't get the Queensland weather show in other states. Despondency took over as she remembered that Tik Tok was worldwide. Callie turned for the door, but a woman rushed in from the back office before she opened it.

'Oh my gawd! It's you!' The squeal filled the room, and Callie froze under the intense stare. 'Oh my gawd, oh my gawd. It really is you. You're famous!'

'I beg your pardon?' Callie tipped her head and gestured to the computer behind the desk. 'I have a booking for tonight.'

'Calista Young?' The girl ran her finger down a page in the open book on the desk.

Callie nodded.

'I recognised your name straight away. I was really hoping it was *the* Calista Young. A cool name, and such a cool thing you did. You're that awesome weather chick who clocked her two-timing boyfriend on TV. Oh my gawd, we've watched it a hundred times, and we cheer you every time. Wait until I tell the girls you're in town,

49

girlfriend! We'll meet you at the pub tonight, for sure.'

Over my dead body, Callie thought as the girl chewed bright pink bubble gum with her mouth open. She didn't look old enough to go to a pub. Despair crawled up Callie's spine. What chance did she have? Even in a tiny town like this in the middle of nowhere, they knew about her. She forced a smile to her face.

'Could you please let me know how much Mr Cartwright paid for my room tonight?'

Once she was checked in, she went to her room, and managed to avoid the receptionist, and the suggested trip to the pub. She rose as soon as it was light the next morning, left the room key in the box outside the office and headed west again.

Chapter 8

Mitchell - Friday

Just after noon, Callie yawned and looked at her watch as she approached a town called Mitchell. A broken night's sleep on a lumpy mattress with something scratching at the walls in the motel at Chinchilla every time she turned the light off had been followed by another long drive. She still had two hundred kilometres to drive until her booked accommodation for tonight and she needed to take a bit of a break before she drove the last leg. As she drove into the small town, a bridge crossed over a pretty river edged with tall lacy-leaved trees, and she noticed a public footpath along the edge of the water. She'd buy some lunch and a coffee, and stretch her legs. Sit by the river and have a rest.

The landscape had changed today; the rolling fields of yellow and green crops around the Darling Downs had gradually changed to paddocks with short scrubby trees and wide expanses of red dirt the further west she drove, but this river was pretty. For the first time, Callie regretted not doing any research on her destination. Her mind had been taken up with the fiasco at the network, and she realised she had to consciously put it behind her.

But despite being very different to the sub-tropical landscapes and huge shady trees she was used to, this landscape held a different beauty.

The door of the bakery opened with a loud creak and the woman behind the counter looked at her curiously; Callie waited for the recognition and the smart comment. As she handed the takeaway coffee over, the woman gestured to her car that she'd parked against the high gutter outside.

'Nice car, love.' Her voice was gravelly as though she'd smoked too many cigarettes in her day.

'Thank you.' Callie handed over twenty dollars and waited for her change.

'You staying in town or just passing through?'

'Just passing through. I'm heading for Augathella.'

The woman handed over the change and shook her head. 'You haven't seen the forecast?'

'No.' Callie flinched and waited for the punchline to follow.

#Wrongforecast.

How many times was she going to have to put up with hearing that before someone else took over the news?

'I haven't.' Her voice was cold as she stared at the woman.

'Well, put your radio on in your car, love. Charleville 603 AM.' The woman folded her arms.

'Just came over the news. Big dust storm heading this way.'

'A dust storm?' Seemed like she'd judged the woman too harshly. Callie smiled as she waited for the reply.

'Yeah. Apparently it's a doozie. You'll want to put the top up on that fancy car of yours, and find yourself a cabin down at the caravan park. The pub's full tonight because the Telstra blokes are in town.'

'Thank you. You really think I should stay here and not keep going? I'm booked into a motel at Augathella tonight.'

'You ever been in a dust storm?'

Callie shook her head. 'No. I'm from Brisbane.'

'Yeah, if you drive into it in that fancy car, you could get stranded on the side of the road. Not much between here and Augathella. Not a good move.'

'Thank you. I'll stay in town here then. Where's the caravan park?'

'Back the way you came into town. On the river just before the bridge.'

'Thank you. I appreciate you telling me.'

'You tell Pat that Rosie said to give you the cabin with the garage. You can put your car away and it won't get scratched when the storm hits. And you won't be stranded in a pile of dirt. '

'Thanks heaps.'

'From the city, aren't ya?'

'I am.'

The woman's grin widened and she chuckled. 'Good to get the "right forecast" for a change, hey love?'

Callie rolled her eyes and hurried out the door. Carefully placing her coffee in the console, she put the soft top up, did a U turn and headed back to the river.

Two hours later, her car was securely away in a fibro garage and she was safely ensconced in a cabin as the afternoon turned to night.

Chapter 9

Kilcoy Station – Saturday

'Daddy, when is our new teacher lady coming to stay?' Nigel kicked the dirt under the clothesline creating a flurry of red dust that settled on the wet white sheets in the washing basket.

Braden flung a double sheet over the outer wire of the Hills Hoist. 'Shit.' Red dust drifted down on the rest of the washing. He'd forgotten about yesterday's dust storm, and hadn't thought to wipe the clothesline first. Not only that, one of the boys had opened the window in the bedroom where he'd been going to put Calista Young, and now it was covered in a thick layer of brown and red dirt. Braden had decided to put her in the donga where Sophie and Jock stayed when they were mustering; they wouldn't need it any more. The nanny would have a bit more privacy there, with her own shower and loo, plus a small kitchen to make a cuppa. It had a nice small veranda along the back that looked out over the house dam.

Yeah, it was a good idea.

'Shit's a bad word, Dad.'

'Sorry, Nigel. Haven't you got a job you should be doing?'

55

'Nuh, I've done them all. I wiped up and put the cups in the cupboard. Rory hasn't done his jobs but. He's on the iPad.'

'No one likes a dobber, mate,' Braden said as he gave up on the washing. He shoved the now dirty wet whites back in the basket to take back to the laundry and put them through the washing machine again. A waste because the tanks were getting low again. The spring rains hadn't arrived yet. 'And to answer your question, the new teacher was staying in town last night, so she should be here before lunch. That's why we want to have the house clean and tidy, and the washing done.'

'Why do we have to have a teacher here? Why can't you drive us to school like Aunty Sophie did?'

'Because I have to go out and work with the cattle.'

'Why? Why can't you pay someone to do that? Uncle Jock said you were rich enough to hire anyone you wanted.'

'Did he now? When did he tell you that?' A slow burn began in Braden's gut.

'No, he didn't talk to us kids. Only to tell us to piss off when he was watching the big TV.'

'Language, Nigel.'

'Fair suck of the sav, Dad. I'm not swearing, I'm only telling you what he said.'

The anger eased as Braden tried not to laugh. *Fair suck of the sav?* Where the hell had that come from? He hoisted the washing basket onto his hip and put his free hand on Nigel's shoulder. 'Come on, we'll go find the other pair.'

'I used to listen to him yelling at Aunty Sophie. Don't tell her that's where I learned all my swear words. He knew lots and lots, Dad. Do you want to hear some?' A cheeky face grinned up at him and a pang of emotion squeezed Braden's heart.

'Hmm, did he? And no, I don't want to hear them. Forget them until you're grown up.'

Petie and Rory were curled up on the lounge together when Braden took a quick look inside on the way to the laundry.

'Five more minutes, men, and then we have some more chores to do after morning tea. You can help me make the bed in the donga and put some milk in the fridge for our nanny.'

Braden was ashamed of the state the house was in. Being there by himself with very few visitors—when Kent came over for a beer, they always sat out on the veranda—had meant the house needed a good spring clean. He hadn't been in the donga since last winter before Jock stayed in it. Sophie had been away in Brisbane for some reason or another, and Jock had kept to himself at night.

The least he could do was have a decent place for Calista Young to stay. Then once she was settled they'd sort out her role. Jeez, he hoped she was happy to cook occasionally.

After Braden put the whites back in the machine—this time they could go in the clothes dryer—he went to the kitchen and filled the kettle.

'Morning tea, guys.'

There was a flurry of bodies through the door and almost before he could blink, the three boys were at the kitchen table.

'Poppers and fruit first, and then if you're still hungry you can have the last of that cake Aunty Sophie made.'

'Will the new nanny make cakes too?' Petie asked.

'I don't know, mate. I have to find out exactly what we can ask her to do.'

Braden put out the drinks and fruit for the boys, and the rest of the cake. He turned a blind eye when they reached for the cake first. Some battles weren't worth fighting. Making a quick cuppa, he snagged the last piece of cake, beating Rory to it by a whisker.

'I've got to go and make a quick phone call, and then we'll all do some work together. If we get it done fast, we might put some of those party pies on for lunch.'

'A party for the new lady, Daddy? Can we have more cake?' Petie's eyes were wide.

'We'll see.' Braden went to the study and dialled Sophie's mobile.

Please be in range, he thought. There was no service outside Augathella for mobiles, and he was sure it would be the same all the way up through Central Queensland. When he'd been mustering on the road, he could remember that occasionally they would come across a small town, or a large property where there was a Telstra tower and they'd all make their phone calls home while they had service for about five kilometres.

He was in luck. Sophie picked up on the second ring.

'Bray, what's wrong? Are the boys all right?' Her voice echoed down the line.

'They're fine. Where are you?'

'Just past Charters Towers. First time we've had service for a few hours.'

'Good timing then. I wanted to ask you a couple of things.'

'Kids are okay?'

'Yes, we've settled into a good routine, although they've nearly eaten all that food you brought over. I wanted to ask you what a nanny does.'

'What do you mean, what she does?'

'Well, you know. Can I ask her to cook? Shop? Make beds? Or is she just here to teach the boys?'

'I don't know, Braden. What did you put in the ad?'

'I dunno. Something about taking their lessons and looking after them. Just general stuff.'

'Well, I guess you're going to have to sit down with her and see what her expectations are. When is she arriving?'

'Some time this morning. As far as I know she should have been in Augathella last night, but we had a pretty bad dust storm on Thursday, so she might have got held up a day.'

'Okay, so when she arrives, sit down and have a good talk and come to an agreement.'

'Okay, I will. You okay, sis? You sound a bit flat.'

'I'm missing the three terrors. Are they really okay? You're not just saying that?'

'No, I'm not. Surprisingly we've coped really well. No major dramas, not too many fights and Petie's slept through every night.'

'Who's he sleeping with?'

Braden chuckled. 'Guess?'

'You?'

'You always were the clever one,' he said.

'Give them all a hug and a kiss from Aunty Soph, will you please, Bray?'

'I will. Take care, Soph. I'll talk to you soon and let you know how the nanny's going.'

'Did you read the rest of my suggestions?'

'No. I haven't had time.'

'Read them, and at least get a housekeeper.'

Braden laughed again. 'Sounds like I need to read it. Take care, Soph. Love you.'

'Love you, too.'

Braden hung the phone up thoughtfully. Sophie sounded unhappy; he knew her well.

Chapter 10

Augathella, Saturday 10am

Callie stayed over in Mitchell and left after breakfast. It had only taken a couple of hours to reach the tiny township of Augathella, and she was pleased that she had navigated a coffee shop and a petrol station with not one iota of recognition. This far west was looking good for her.

Anonymity, that was what she wanted. She was now Callie Young, ex-school teacher and governess or nanny or whatever the position was she had taken up. It was all very vague, and her thoughts hadn't been focused when she'd applied. She'd had the interview, accepted the job and taken off.

In *her* car.

As she'd packed the car after the non-eventful car retrieval the night before, she'd left after having a wine with Jen, her phone had pinged with an incoming text.

From Greg.

She read the first few abusive words, then closed the message and deleted it. And took much satisfaction deleting him from her contact list.

Her anger was directed inwards; she had been so gullible.

No more. From now on, she was her own boss and no one was going to tell her what to do with her life. Or her car. Or her career.

As Callie drove through the morning and closer to her destination, a niggle of uncertainty began to tug at her.

The isolation and the vastness of the landscape was not what she'd expected. After she'd turned north at a small town called Morven the traffic had almost disappeared. Occasionally she would overtake a four wheel drive vehicle towing a caravan.

She shook her head. People actually came out here for holidays? For pleasure?

Each of the caravans had a call sign on the back, and the signs made her smile.

Val and Ron. Give us a call on Channel 18.

Harry and Marge. Adventure before Dementia. Channel 40.

Peter and Cheryl. If the van's a rocking, call the police. It's not us. She'd chuckled at that one as she'd followed the vans into Augathella. She'd parked the car and gone for a walk to stretch her legs and delay her imminent arrival at *Kilcoy Station*.

The giant meat ant sculpture in the park at Augathella made her grin too. She'd heard of the

Big Banana and seen the Big Pineapple. But a Big Meat Ant?

Hmmm. Where the hell had she ended up?

After leaving the park, Callie did as much shopping as she could in the newsagent and grocery store she found in the small row of shops in the main street. She'd packed some curriculum materials, but hadn't given any thought to what supplies her students might—or might not—have. Her lessons were still on a hard drive attached to her laptop, and she'd packed her printer for printing out worksheets. Pens and pencils, and some exercise books and stickers would be enough to get started until she saw where they were up to. She'd been in such a state before she'd left Brisbane, she hadn't even asked how many children, how old they were or what sex.

Not that it mattered. She'd taught from prep to Grade 6 when she'd started out as a teacher and even though she'd been out of it for a while, she could summon up her curriculum knowledge quickly. Excited anticipation replaced the nervous niggle; it would be good to be teaching again.

Callie left town at the western end, following Braden Cartwright's instructions and took the south western route on the Charleville road. After seven kilometres, she turned again onto another road, relieved when she saw a sign that said *Kilcoy Station*, twenty-two kilometres.

Almost there—she should make it by lunchtime. Biting her lip, she realised it would have been polite to call and let them know she would arrive today. Pulling over on the soft red dirt at the side of the road, she took out her phone, and dialled the number but there was no answer. She left a brief message: "Callie Young here. See you in an hour or two."

She set off again but the state of the road began to make her nervous. She'd never been on a road like this before; ungraded and so corrugated her car bumped and slewed left and right even when she was going really slowly.

She'd left Augathella with the top down, but as the sun rose higher in the sky, her scalp began to burn, and she pulled over to put the soft top up. As she pulled over to the side, there was a large thump, and she got out to see what it was.

Walking around the car, she sussed it out and there was no sign of any damage, but Callie almost cried when she saw how dirty her usually shiny red sports car was. Hopefully she'd be able to wash it, although the dry cracked riverbed she'd crossed at the edge of town made her wonder about the water situation out here.

She straightened her shoulders, got back in, and pushed the button to bring the soft top up so she wouldn't burn, but nothing happened. Pressing it again, she frowned and then started the car, and tried to get the top up again.

Nothing.

With a sigh, she reached into the back for the red and white striped bandana that matched her T-shirt and wound it around her head. It was getting awfully hot; the sun had burned her legs below the cuffed leg of her white shorts already. The condition of the road improved for a while, and Callie drove another twelve kilometres before a loud clunking started.

Clunk, clunk, clunk.

She slowed the car down to a crawl and tipped her head to the side. There was definitely something wrong. With the car, that was. As well as the situation she had found herself in. She tried to ignore the noise for a while, telling herself she was within ten kilometres of her destination. Ahead, the road was a straight unbroken line of red, and in the far distance she could see a line of low blue mountains to the south west. Low tussocky trees were scattered in the red sandy soil as far as she could see.

But there was no sign of life. No cars. No houses. No cattle. No wildlife of any kind to be seen. For a moment, fear tugged at her; it was the first time in her life she had been alone in the true sense of the word. At the same time, the noise coming from beneath the car got louder and suddenly the driver's side dipped and there was a loud wrenching noise.

'Well, Calista Young,' she said, trying to inject some courage into her voice. 'I guess this is what you call a breakdown.'

Reaching across for her bag, she pulled out her RACQ membership card, and her phone. The garage back at Augathella had the RACQ sign out the front. Squinting in the bright light, Callie dialled the number on the card and waited.

And waited.

Waited for any sound at all. Her phone was dead. With a frown, she put her hand over her eyes and looked at the screen. The service icons had disappeared. It was the first time they'd ever been completely missing from the screen.

Either her phone was dead, or there was no phone service out here.

In either case, she was in trouble. There was obviously not going to be any traffic along this road, so there was only one course of action open to her.

Callie sat there for a moment biting her lip, then turned the key and looked at the digital odometer reading. It had been twenty-two kilometres from the turn off to the *Kilcoy Station*, and by her calculations she had come at least seventeen of them.

So at worst, she had a five kilometre walk ahead of her. A walk on a dirt road, in forty degree heat, without a proper hat.

At least she had plenty of water.

Okay, she'd moved to the outback. She needed a survival kit to get her to the farmhouse or the station or whatever it was called.

Leaning over her seat, she opened her suitcase on the back seat and pulled out her nylon backpack. She threw in her purse and phone, a change of undies, a clean pair of shorts and a T-shirt, her toothbrush, and two bottles of water. The small amount of food she'd bought at the grocery store wasn't perishable so it could stay. Reaching for her makeup bag, she pulled out the lipstick that matched her red nails and outlined her lips. She would not turn up looking like a hobo.

For a couple of minutes before she set off, Callie stood beside the car and frowned; she looked long and hard at her laptop. It was too bulky to carry. Weighing up the risk of leaving it on the seat in the burning sun, and in full view of anyone who might come past against the hassle of carrying it for an unknown distance, she tried to decide what to do.

In the end she slipped the external hard drive into her backpack. If the worst came to the worst, she'd still have her files. Surely the laptop would be right out here until the Cartwrights could bring her back to the car to get her stuff.

With a frown, she realised if anyone else came past they could help themselves to everything in the car. Her two suitcases, and her laptop.

No, she wasn't going to risk it.

Taking care to watch where she walked— although her white high top converse sneakers were soon as red as the dust on the road—Callie walked into the scrub at the side of the road. Over a slight rise and about thirty metres from the car there was a wide ditch. She turned and looked back to the road. Unless you walked over the slight rise, you'd never know the ditch was there.

She hurried back to the car, retrieved her two suitcases, slung her laptop bag around her neck and carried them over. She carefully placed them on this side of the ditch under a slight bank. There, the worst that could happen now was that her car would get stolen, but there was little chance of that happening because the wheels wouldn't turn. Hopefully the Cartwrights could bring her straight back here and she could retrieve her belongings quickly.

Callie looked up at the clear blue sky and figured it wasn't going to rain. The only problem would be the sun on her laptop. She rearranged her two suitcases, standing them up and putting the laptop bag in the shade between them. Pocketing the car keys, she slipped the backpack over her shoulders, tightened the bandanna around her head and headed back to the road.

The road was straight and red as far as she could see. Presumably there'd be a gate or a sign to turn off to *Kilcoy Station*. She took a deep drink from her water bottle—the water was already lukewarm—and set off down the road towards her new job.

The sun was unbearably hot on her head, perspiration trickled down her arms and legs, and red dust covered her shoes. As she walked, Callie summoned up and muttered every swear word she could think of and applied them to Greg.

Her mood and language worsened and Callie's cursing was the only sound until a huge crow flew from the high branches of a gum tree. It cawed at her as it swooped close to the road and glared at her scathingly.

'Don't mess with me,' she yelled as she glared back. She hated bloody crows; she had done ever since she'd read that Merlin book by that New Age author guy. She couldn't even remember the name of the author or the book, but she'd hated crows ever since. Callie shuddered as she remembered the story had started in a roadside ditch.

Hopefully it wasn't an omen.

Nevertheless, the interaction with the crow took her mind off snakes, wild buffalos, vultures, and any other life-threatening creatures she could encounter on her walk in this arid and remote outback. She kept a close eye on the crow until it flew away with one loud raucous squawk.

Callie pulled out her phone and took a video of the landscape as she walked, using some not quite so rude words to express what she thought of Greg Broadbent at this moment. Words that were suitable for recording and for the ears of her friends who would be waiting to hear that she had arrived safely. She'd send it off as soon as she had service and she knew that Jen would reply straight away, with a **Come Home**!

Maybe she'd do her own Tik Tok video one day and call it Life after a— no, she couldn't put *that* word on social media.

Revenge was a sweet thing. Her imagination kept her mind off her current predicament as she strode west. Her mood improved with every step.

The same *couldn't* be said for her appearance, she thought as perspiration trickled down her arms and legs.

Chapter 11

Kilcoy Station – Saturday 1pm

After the boys had eaten the party pies Braden found in the freezer—thanks, Soph—he looked around the kitchen, satisfied with how it looked.

A glimmer of guilt lingered. It hadn't looked this clean and sparkly for a long time. Over the past months, his habit had been to wash up on Sunday nights to clear the way for the coming week. That was about it. There was no need to clean up, because he was the only one who ever saw it. But today. . .

Pretty spiff.

No cattle drench on the bench tops, no bits and pieces that usually accumulated through the week. You could actually see the grey and white marble swirl colour of the benchtops and they were gleaming.

For the first time in a long time, Braden smiled as he thought of what Julia would have said.

Just what he'd thought.

Pretty spiff, love. He could almost hear her voice, and the usual grief didn't slam in.

'Dad, what's happening?' Nigel stood in the doorway with a cranky face. 'Rory said I can't turn the TV on.'

'What's happening is that we're going to town to get a few more groceries before the new teacher lady arrives. You've eaten almost all the food Aunty Sophie cooked.' He looked up at the clock with a frown.

He hoped the new nanny hadn't changed her mind; it was after one already, and he thought she would have been here before midday.

'Okay. Can we have hot chips in town?'

Braden opened his mouth to tell his son that they'd just demolished a whole box of party pies, but he bit his tongue. 'Sounds like a good arvo treat to me, Nige. Go and get your brothers. Tell them it's time to go.'

Ten minutes later, Braden and the three boys were in the twin cab ute. It was the first time they'd left the house since Sophie had dropped them off.

Braden was almost to the cattle grid near the main gate when he remembered that he'd meant to turn the pump on to bring some water down from the artesian bore to top up the tanks.

'Shit,' he muttered and immediately regretted it as giggles came from the back seat.

73

'Daddy said "shit" again,' Nigel said with glee. There'd been a few occasions this week when his language had been noted. And always by Nigel.

'I'm sorry. Forget I said that,' Braden said as he turned back to the shed.

'Aw, Dad, aren't we going to town now?' Rory whined.

'Yes, we are. But I have to turn the pump on. Just wait there.' He left the car running, jumped out and hurried across to the main pump switch and turned it on. By the time they got back, the water would have come down the channel to the garden tanks and he could put the sprinklers on and give the lawn—such as it was—and the gardens, a good soaking. The place would look a bit brighter. He was going to do everything he could to keep this nanny here.

Braden frowned; that was if she was okay. If she was okay, and then if he got himself organised over the weekend, he might even get the pool cleaned and filled.

'Right, men! Let's get to town and find this new teacher lady.'

Chapter 12

Callie's feet hurt—her Converse walking shoes appeared to be made more for appearance than comfort. Greg had insisted she buy a matching pair to his for when they went for their walk along Moreton Bay before breakfast on Sunday mornings. They were rubbing, her toes were stinging, and that was only half the problem. Her neck and arms were a lather of perspiration, and her throat was as dry as—

She stopped feeling sorry for herself and stared ahead intently as a puff of red dust appeared in the distance. It looked like she was about to be passed by a car. The first one she'd seen since she'd driven out of Augathella an hour ago.

Callie moved to the side of the road, reached up and retied her bandana, and then took a swig of water while she waited. Water trickled down her chin and she grimaced as she wiped it away and her hand came away red.

As the vehicle approached, she could see it was some sort of high farm ute. She straightened her back as the dust-covered twin cab slowed and parked in the middle of the road.

'Gidday there, you've taken a wrong turn,' a deep voice called to her. The guy who had his elbow half out of the open window looked at her curiously. 'No point hitchhiking on this road. It doesn't go anywhere and you won't see any other cars come by. Lucky we were heading to town. Do you want a lift back to the highway? We're heading that way.'

She stared at him, but he continued talking before she could reply. 'There's not a lot of room, but we can fit you in if you don't mind a squeeze.'

Finally she found her voice. 'No, but thank you very much for the offer. I do need to keep going this way. I'm expected at *Kilcoy Station*.'

***

Braden frowned as the sweaty, dust-covered woman replied politely, her voice posh, and her words clearly articulated. He stared at her, looked more closely and then shook his head.

No. No way. It couldn't be the nanny.

This young woman was nothing like he'd expected.

'Why are you hitching to Kilcoy?' he asked carefully.

'I'm hitching because my car broke down about three kilometres back, and they were expecting me there a couple of hours ago. A Braden Cartwright.'

'Shit,' he muttered as he realised she *was* the nanny.

'Dad said shit,' Petie squealed with delight.

Braden opened the ute door and jumped out to stand next to the woman. At the same time Nigel and Rory leaned out the driver's window.

'Is that our new teacher lady, Dad?' Rory asked.

Nigel was out to impress in his inimitable way. 'What's all that red shit on her lips?'

Braden turned and roared. 'Nigel Cartwright! That's it. You've been warned. No more television for you for a week.'

The girl took a step back. '*You're* Braden Cartwright?' she said, staring at him with horror on her face.

Braden took a deep breath. 'Sorry I yelled, but yes, I am.'

Her hands went to her hips and he wondered if it was to draw attention to her lithe figure and fancy clothes.

'Now just wait one moment. I didn't think you had television out here,' their new nanny said, rolling eye-linered and mascaraed eyes. 'That's it. I've had more than enough today. Just take me back to my car, and I'll organise to get towed into town.'

'Just a minute. Look, I'm sorry, just wait.' Embarrassment flooded through Braden. 'Let's start again.' He gestured with a sharp jerk of his hand for

77

the boys to stop hanging out the window, before he held out his hand to her.

'I'm assuming you're Calista Young. Welcome to *Kilcoy Station*. I'm Braden Cartwright. I apologise for my son's rudeness, I apologise for my reaction to his swearing, and no, we don't have television out here. The kids watch DVDs on the television.'

Although why the hell television, or her preference for not having one, was so important to her accepting the job, beat him. Maybe she was into some kind of weird religion.

Her expression cleared slightly as she lifted her hand and pushed back a stray strand of dark hair that had fallen from beneath the striped fabric wound around her head.

'Okay, I'm sorry too. I'm tired and hot and sweaty.' She reached out and shook his hand. 'And yes, I'm Callie Young. Nice to meet you.'

Braden held back a groan; her fingernails were like talons and painted the same red as the lipstick outlining her full lips.

The nanny? A teacher? Maybe he should have looked at her application and references, and not left it up to that woman in Brisbane.

He had no one else to blame but himself. This one looked like she should grace the front page of a fashion magazine, and not be in the remote outback teaching his three boys.

But Braden tried to be fair. There was no point prejudging her. He'd learned that before, but it was still a bad habit of his. And besides, they needed her. Today.

He turned to the car and glanced into the back. Petie had drifted off. He lowered his voice. 'Rory, Nigel, get in the back with Petie. Now.' Although quiet, his tone held a warning note, and both the boys were smart enough to pick up on it. 'And keep quiet and still. Don't wake him up.'

Petie had had a rough night, and because he'd slept in Braden's bed again, so had Braden. That was one of the reasons he was short-tempered today. Lack of sleep, worry about the muster, and some niggles of concern about Sophie after listening to what the boys had said about Jock.

What was it the experts said? *Out of the mouths of babes.*

'Come around and jump in the front, Ms Young. I'll take you back to your car, and we'll pick up your luggage, and have a quick look at the car. I assume you have luggage with you?'

'Callie, please. I do, but I took my two cases, and my laptop out of the car. I didn't want them to be stolen.'

'Where are they?' He looked at the side of the road where she'd been waiting, but there was nothing there.

79

'I put them in a ditch just off the road, away from my car.'

'There's no fear of that on our road. It doesn't lead anywhere apart from our station, so there's no through traffic. The occasional truck does—' Suddenly her words registered. 'Hang on, what did you say? You put them in a ditch?'

She nodded.

'How wide a ditch? How far from the road?'

An elegant shrug. 'Around thirty metres.'

'Quick, run! Get in the car.' He grabbed her arm, and pushed her as gently as he could towards the passenger side.

'Bloody hell, Dad. You're gonna be in trouble.' Nigel's voice came from the back seat as she climbed into the passenger seat.'

'Zip it, Nigel, and that's two weeks with no TV now.'

As soon as the passenger door closed, Braden pushed the clutch in, changed into second gear, and planted his foot on the accelerator.

'What's the matter?' Her glare was as cold as the posh voice. 'Where are we going?'

'The drain is an irrigation channel.'

'It's okay. There was no water in it,' she said smartly.

'That's right,' Braden said as he crunched into third gear. 'It would have been dry an hour ago but I

80

turned the main pump on back at the house when we left.'

'It's okay. My car is about five kilometres from the house, or at least that's what I worked out from your sign.'

He tried to keep his tone patient as he explained how the irrigation channels worked. 'The water is tapped from the artesian basin below us, and it services many of our cattle stations. Our garden tanks are a bit low, so before we left I turned the pump on. That feeds our water from the bore through the channel along the side of the road to the station. It travels about ten kilometres before it gets to our place.'

'But the drain was bone dry.' Her voice wasn't as confident now. 'It looked like it had never had water in it.'

He flicked a glance at her. 'It only takes a couple of forty degree days to dry it out and crack the mud here. How long ago did you put your stuff in the drain?'

She frowned and looked down at the expensive watch that was on her now sunburned wrist. 'About twenty minutes ago. At most.'

'You might be lucky. The water mightn't have reached it yet.' Braden changed gears and accelerated harder. The wheels spun, and then after the tyres got traction the twin cab lurched up and down the corrugations. 'It's pretty dry, so it'll take a while to come to the surface and make its way down the channel.'

He tried to sound positive, but the first three kilometres of channel had a concrete base and sides and the water would gain momentum in that first bit before it turned to a dirt channel.

Braden peered ahead and after a few minutes a low red car appeared on the side of the road in the far distance. That'd be right. Fire engine red to match her nails, lipstick and clothes.

'That's my car just up there.' She pointed to the vehicle he'd already spotted.

A bloody sports car. He kept his face expressionless and didn't comment.

Stretching high in his seat Braden glanced to the side of the road. 'The water hasn't come this far yet. You might be in luck. But we'd better be quick. It won't be far off.'

'How deep does it get?'

He turned his head and stared at her. 'Over a metre.'

She looked away from him and didn't say another word.

Two minutes later the ute slewed to a stop.

'I can hear it coming,' Braden said as he pulled the hand brake on and flung his door open. 'Nigel, Rory. Come with me, and watch out for snakes.

Callie—Miss Young—please stay here and keep an eye on Petie for me.'

He didn't wait for her answer as he took off towards the irrigation channel.

Chapter 13

Callie opened her mouth to answer her new boss, but before she could speak he and the two little boys had taken off and disappeared behind the slight rise in the scrub.

Petie? Who was Petie? She'd spent the last five minutes staring ahead as the ute had gone tearing back along the dirt road she'd walked.

Now she turned to the back seat for the first time as a noise came from the seat behind her, and her gaze settled on a little boy in a booster seat set in the middle. He was staring at her and his face crumpled with distress as she stared back.

'Oh, please don't cry, sweetie. Are you Petie?'

Stupid question, Callie. There was no one else in the back seat.

'Where's my Daddy? Are you the teacher lady?'

'Daddy had to go and get my bag.' Callie pulled a face. 'Because I left it in the drain and it might be wet. Will we go and see if he saved it?' He nodded slowly, but his face was wary. 'And my name's Callie, and yes, I'm the teacher lady.'

'Yes, find Daddy.'

She unclipped the seat belt and opened her door, looking down to check the ground was clear before she jumped into the red dust.

Braden Cartwright's warning to his other two boys about snakes hadn't gone unheeded.

The red dirt was clear, but her brows drew together in a frown as she looked at the side of the road and saw some slithery marks. They certainly weren't footprints. She'd get the little boy out of the back before he started to cry, and they'd be very careful as they walked over to see if her bags had been saved. She looked over to the scrub, but there was no sign of the boys or their father. She shivered as she thought about how she had walked through there before without really watching where she was going. Greg had been in her head; she had to get over her anger.

Opening the back door, she reached over and tried to find the clip that secured the belt into the seat, but she couldn't see it.

'Hang on a minute, Petie, silly Callie can't find the seatbelt.'

His little giggle made her smile. 'Silly Callie,' he repeated.

'Yep, silly Callie, who put her bags in the drain, and silly Callie who can't undo your seatbelt.'

A little hand grabbed hers as she felt along the side of the seat.

85

'This side, silly Callie.' He pulled her hand over his legs and let go when her fingers encountered the belt holder.

'Ah, thank you.'

With a loud click, the catch let go, and Petie leaned forward in the seat.

'Can you get out or will I lift you out?' she asked, holding her hands out to the little boy who wasn't much bigger than a toddler. In a flash he slid off the seat and ducked under her arm and was out the door. Another puff of red dust filled the air as he landed in the dirt.

'Okay, so you know how to get out.'

He waited beside the ute. 'I'm a big boy. I'll be four on my birthday.'

'I'm pleased to hear that.' Callie held out her hand. 'Come on. We'll go find your dad and the others.'

He looked up at her. 'Carry me, please. Daddy said snakes. I don't like snakes. They bite and bite you hard.'

Callie shivered again and wiped her damp hands on the side of her once white shorts, reached down and swung him into her arms. At least she'd had toddler experience with Jen's kids, and he was almost kinder age. She knew how to deal with kids that age with her eyes shut almost. By the look of things, she'd only have two boys to teach; Petie was too young for the classroom by a good two years.

But it would be fun having a little one around; she'd loved minding her friends' kids.

Any chance she might have of having her own kids was gone; she was going to ignore that ticking biological clock. She would never trust a man again.

Petie sat comfortably on her hip with one hand holding her shoulder as she turned towards the scrub where the ditch was.

'Look, there's Daddy.'

Callie followed the direction he was pointing and a jolt of worry hit her. She could just see the top of her employer's head through the low trees as he ran along the side of the ditch about a hundred metres along from where they were parked. There was no sign of the two boys.

'Uh oh. Not looking good,' she said with a groan. Could the day get any worse?

***

Braden scrambled up the bank, one suitcase in his hand and the laptop case under his arm. He'd managed to get them out of the channel with about thirty seconds to spare as the first surge of water had come down from the bore. He put the suitcase and the laptop bag on the ground in front of the boys. 'Don't move, you pair. Wait right there.'

'Look, Dad. There's another one!' Rory leaned over the bank.

'It's floating, like a boat!' Nigel yelled, excitement in his voice.

'I'll get it. And don't go near the water. Guard them.' By the time Braden had thrown the suitcase and the laptop up to the boys, the water was up to his thighs and the other suitcase had started its journey along the irrigation channel.

He raced along the edge of the channel, his work boots squelching as he kept his eyes on the other suitcase as it bobbed along on top of the quickly rising water. If it sank, they'd have no hope of finding it.

Braden was out of breath when the handle snagged against a dead tree that had fallen across the channel about three hundred metres along. From up here it looked as though the tree trunk was broad enough for him to shinny along so he wouldn't have to go into the water to reach the suitcase and get any wetter than he already was. He scrambled down the bank again; the dirt was softer here and his boots slipped the last metre, and he grabbed one of the protruding branches just in time to stop himself falling into the now-deep water.

He tested the stability of the tree trunk with one foot and it didn't budge, so he dropped down into a crouch and inched along the tree with his arm stretched out for the red—*of course it was bloody red*—suitcase.

'Got it,' he muttered as his fingers closed over the handle. At the same time there was an ominous creak and the trunk rolled beneath him.

Braden kept a firm grip on the handle of the suitcase as he slid beneath the muddy water, and took a deep breath as the weight of the suitcase pulled him under.

Of all the stupid places to put her stuff.

What sort of idiot put luggage and computers in an irrigation channel? He kicked hard, and as his head broke the surface a Coke can and an empty chip packet floated past, worsening his already bad mood. Even this far out of town, there was rubbish in the channel.

Determined not to let go of the suitcase now that he had hold of it, he let the water take him along until the bottom of the channel rose and he could feel solid ground beneath his feet. He moved across and hoisted the red suitcase up the bank. As he clambered after it, he noticed the Louis Vuitton insignia on the side, and an engraved name plate that said G. Broadbent.

Who was this woman?

His thoughts boiled and he cursed Sophie as he tried to climb the bank in his sodden boots. This nanny person had turned up in a low-slung sports car, with her long red talons and colour co-ordinated clothes and designer shoes. Expensive luggage that had someone else's name on it.

How did he even know he could trust her? How did he even know she was who she said she was? The first thing he'd be doing would be asking for some sort of ID. And more fool him, he'd left the three boys back there where she was. And the keys in the ute.

All she'd have to do would be offer hot chips and the boys would be in the ute with her in a flash.

The curse that came from his lips was the worst yet, but Nigel wasn't in earshot. It took two attempts to get to the top of the bank and by the time he succeeded, his long pants were streaked with red mud, his boots were damn near totalled, and his mood was as filthy as his boots.

Braden focused on his breathing as he trudged back along the track at the top of the channel. He would keep it together until he and Miss Whoever She Was Callie Young could have a conversation in private. He didn't want to upset the boys.

'Dad! You got it.' Nigel and Rory were standing where he had told them to wait fifty metres away. *She* was beside them.

Braden frowned and broke into a loping run, as best as he could with his boots slipping up and down, and the damn suitcase slapping against his legs. It felt like it was full of bricks; it was a wonder the damn thing had floated. He'd told her to wait in the car with Petie. She wouldn't know that the little terror could undo his belt by himself, and that he had a fascination with water.

'Where's Petie?' he yelled, scanning the channel as he ran.

She turned as he called and relief surged though him as he realised that she was holding Petie on one hip. His red T-shirt had blended with her red shirt from a distance.

'He's here, Dad,' Rory called back.

'Thanks, mate.' Braden lifted his spare hand and acknowledged Rory's call. 'Stay calm,' he muttered to himself. 'Shit.'

And watch your language.

Chapter 14

Callie's heart sank when she saw the tight smile on Braden Cartwright's face. He looked decidedly unimpressed, not to mention very wet. His hair was sticking up in spikes where he'd run his muddy hand through it. The last thing she wanted or needed was a cranky boss.

She injected a bright note into her voice, and plastered a wide smile on her face. 'Thank you *so* much. I really appreciate what you've done.'

He nodded. 'I'm sorry one got wet. We weren't quick enough.'

'No, it's fine. Totally my fault for putting my luggage in an irrigation channel. My first outback lesson.' Callie waved a dismissive hand. 'Anyway if one of them had to get wet, that was the best one.'

'Why, because it's not yours?' His expression held disdain, and she knew he was thinking less of her by the minute. He'd obviously seen Greg's name on it.

'Yes, they're both mine. I meant because there were winter clothes in that one and they'll wash and dry out by next winter.' As soon as the words left her mouth she regretted them. It sounded like she had decided to stay for the long term without even knowing anything about the job, or the boss and his wife, and the kids. Or seeing if she was suitable to her new employer.

She glanced down at Petie still snug on her hip; so far the three children had been polite and well behaved. If you discounted the comment about her lipstick.

Early days, Callie. If it didn't feel right, she could leave. She didn't owe the Cartwright family anything and so far she was as unimpressed with Braden as he seemed to be with her.

The man occupying her thoughts held out his arms to Petie but the little boy shook his head. 'No, Daddy, you is muddy. I like Callie.'

That brought an eyebrow raise.

'Okay, then. Let's get back to the ute. We can take Miss Young to the donga and she can get sorted while I have a shower.' He turned to Callie. 'I'll come back and sort out your car later.'

'That's not fair, Dad!' The boy, Nigel, stamped his foot. 'We were going to get hot chips in town.'

'Sometimes, mate, circumstances change and we have to adapt.' To his credit, the father's voice was calm.

Nigel started to bellow. 'I want hot chips.'

This time it was Callie who raised her eyebrows, but she walked over to the angry little boy, and put her hand on his shoulder. 'I'm sorry, Nigel, it was my fault for being silly.'

93

'Silly Callie,' Petie echoed.

Nigel looked up and glared at her. 'It is your fault and *you* can bloody well fix it.'

Callie's mouth dropped open, and she wasn't sure how to reply; she didn't have to as Braden looked over at the older boy. He gestured to the laptop bag. 'Are you right to carry that for us, Rory?'

'Yes, Dad.'

Nigel's squeal pierced the still air as his father reached down, picked him up and threw him over his shoulder like a sack of potatoes. 'You and I will have a talk back at the house.'

It was a silent group who trudged back along the track to the twin cab ute. Callie carried Petie, Rory carried the laptop, and she was most impressed as Braden carried a suitcase in each hand with his son over one shoulder. Her thoughts were in a whirl; this wasn't the way she had expected to arrive and be greeted at the cattle station. But at least it wasn't a public humiliation and she could cope. Her car breakdown and then putting her bags in an irrigation channel hadn't been witnessed by the whole world. Okay, so her new boss might think she was a ditz, but she could cope with that. It was better than being seen as a bitch by a million or so viewers.

They reached the ute and Braden put the suitcases down, and Nigel slid to the ground. He stood there looking mutinous. Opening the back door, Braden held his arms out for Petie. 'Rory. You go around the other side and get in. Nigel, you wait until Petie's strapped in and get in this side. I don't want to hear one more word from you until we have a little talk in my office.'

Callie opened the front door and climbed into the passenger seat while both suitcases and laptop were loaded into the back of the ute. She had taken the suitcases from Greg's apartment when she and Jen had gone there earlier in the week.

Greg had found the copycat Louis Vuitton luggage online the week before they'd gone to Pentecost Island, and he'd asked her to pay for them because he'd been a bit short that week.

'I'll pay you back next week,' he'd said.

Pah! There were a lot of things that Greg had said and done that she should have taken as a warning.

He'd never paid her back the seven hundred and fifty dollars so the suitcases belonged to her. The anger that bubbled briefly as she thought about her lowlife ex disappeared when Braden Cartwright opened the ute door.

Callie's mouth dried and she pushed away the totally inappropriate thoughts and reaction that slammed through her.

He'd removed his sodden boots and socks, *and* his wet shirt. Her eyes moved up from his bare feet and settled on a broad tanned chest.

She swallowed and looked away as heat filled her cheeks. Not only broad and tanned, but he was absolutely built. The only place she'd ever seen a perfect specimen like that was in her dreams.

She couldn't help the grin that tugged at her lips. Although there had been that time Jen and Nat had dragged her to that male stripper troupe show for Kristie's hen's night. Braden Cartwright would have fitted right in.

Callie stared straight ahead as he started the ute, not game to turn and look at him in case her eyes dropped to that gorgeous chest again.

For God's sake, wake up to yourself! She closed her eyes and chastised herself.

She'd already presented herself badly enough without salivating over a married man *and* father, before they'd even arrived at the cattle station.

Besides being totally inappropriate, she firmly reminded herself, she was off men for good.

For life. They were not to be trusted.

##

The wheels of the ute rattled over a metal grid when they reached a locked gate at the end of another long straight road. Callie stared at a large sign warning that *Kilcoy Station* was private property.

Braden pulled up. 'Rory. Your turn.' It was the first time he'd spoken since they'd set off, and Callie was finding the silence uncomfortable, but she'd be damned if she was going to break it first. The occasional sniff had come from the back seat and she wondered if Nigel was crying. Even though he was a naughty boy, her heart went out to him. When she'd been teaching, it only took tears to soften her, and the naughtier kids in the class had soon picked up on that. She'd try not to do that here: Nigel was obviously a handful.

The passenger side back door of the ute opened and Rory ran to the gate, unlooped the chain and pushed the gate back and Braden drove them through.

'We're almost to the house,' Braden said as he waited for Rory to shut the gate and get back in the car. 'We have the gates to keep the cattle out of the house yard.'

'Where do you do the milking?' Callie kept her eyes ahead, feeling embarrassed as she wondered if he'd noticed her eyes widen when she'd looked at his chest.

Oh God, how embarrassing.

A rude splutter came from the back seat, and Braden raised a warning finger. 'Nigel.'

'Ah, we don't have a dairy, we raise cattle for meat,' he said. 'Plus we breed bulls.'

'Okay.'

Soon a house came into view and Callie's eyes widened again when she saw the size of it. A long one-storey brick house with a high-pitched green roof sat in the middle of a large fenced-off block. It was one of the biggest houses she'd ever seen. High colonial windows broke the brick every few metres and she wondered how many rooms could be in a house that size. On the other side of the fence was a large shed with the same green roof. Callie looked around, taking in the rest of the buildings scattered around the paddocks past the house. As they got closer, she was surprised to see the mess covering the dead lawn. Old drums and various pieces of equipment sat on the dry brown grass.

'Dad, I need the dunny.' Nigel unclipped the seat belt and leaned over the back of his father's seat. 'I'm in a hurry.'

'Okay, Nigel and Rory, you can both jump out now. I won't be long.' He flicked a glance at her. 'Then I'll drop Callie over to the donga.' Braden's voice interrupted her perusal of the property; it was very different to what she'd expected.

'Okay, thank you,' she said slowly, wondering if she would look stupid again if she asked what a donga was.

Then again, she had no experience of the outback, so maybe huge houses on cattle stations like this one were the norm.

And dongas, whatever they were.

As they stopped at the back of the house where the yard was much tidier, she spotted two small buildings across the dead grass about a hundred metres from the house.

'We have two dongas and they're both empty at the moment,' he explained.

Callie nodded. *Donga, okay, some sort of apartment.*

'Ms Young will come back over and see you in a while. You can show her the schoolroom and your rooms.'

Flicking a quick glance into the back seat, Callie regretted it straight away when Nigel poked his tongue out when she turned to look at him. The two boys jumped out of the car and pounded up the back steps. The screen door banged shut behind them and there was silence.

She stared after them, her heart sinking. This was going to be an interesting job. Nigel was obviously a strong-willed kid and Callie wondered what the parents' discipline was like. There'd been no sign of Mrs Cartwright yet. Braden hadn't mentioned his wife, and no one had come out to meet the car.

Maybe she was away, but she'd thought he would have mentioned that. She was pleased that she had separate accommodation at least. Jen was right; she should have found out more about the setup out here before she'd taken off from the city.

'Get yourself settled in and unpack while I have a shower. Anything you want to wash from your suitcase, put aside and I'll show you where the laundry is in the main house when you come over.'

'Okay.'

'I checked the one with the single bedroom for you. When the muster starts, we'll use the other one with two bedrooms to put up some of the contract staff.'

'Thank you.'

'Being here will give you a bit of privacy and means you don't have to be in the house. You won't feel like you're on duty all the time. Plus—' he grinned and glanced over to the back seat where Petie had started to sing a song about baby sharks at the top of his voice— 'It'll give you a break from the three terrors.'

'Yes, we need to have a talk about what you expect,' Callie said as he pulled up near the steps of a building with unpainted timber walls. A white front door was flanked by two dust covered windows. A single white plastic chair sat on the veranda.

'Yeah, we do. Once you get settled come on over to the house and we'll have a chat. I don't expect you to start today. You'll be tired after the drive from Brisbane.'

'Okay. How long before you'll be ready to meet with me?'

'Give me half an hour.'

Callie frowned. It was all "me", no mention of an "us".

'There's tea and coffee in the cupboard in your kitchen, and some fresh milk in the fridge. Towels in the bathroom and if you want the air conditioner on, the remote's in the top drawer in the kitchen. I hope it's clean enough. It didn't look too bad when I brought the milk over and made the bed. You can tell me if there's any problems or if there's anything else you need when you come over.'

Still no mention of a wife.

'Okay.' Callie reached for the car door handle. She looked across at him and kept her eyes away from his bare chest as he opened his door too. She didn't think he'd done that on purpose. She hoped not anyway. His shirt had been sodden.

'I'm sorry I caused you a hassle today,' she said. 'Please don't worry about going out to my car again. I'll call the RACQ later. There is phone service here, isn't there?'

For the first time, his face creased in a genuine smile and she thought what a good looking man he was. Rugged and tanned, but he had a nice face. Kind.

Braden got out and walked around to her side of the car. 'Ah, sort of. We hook up via satellite, so I'll try to get your mobile and computer connected to our network later. If we can't get you set up, there's a house phone hooked up to the satellite. You're quite welcome to use that whenever you need to.'

'Oh, okay.' She picked up her small backpack and turned, sliding her legs down the side of the seat, and jumped to the ground next to him. 'See you in a while, Petie.'

She waited at the bottom of the four steps while Braden took her two suitcases and laptop case from the back of the ute. He carried them up to the veranda.

When he came back down the steps, Callie looked past him and stepped back so he could get past her to his ute. 'Is there a front door key?' she asked.

'No. They're never locked. Don't worry, it's safe out here. We never lock doors.'

Hmm, she thought, not very happy with the idea of not being able to lock her door at night.

'Okay, I guess I'm used to the city. I'll have to get used to being in the outback.'

'If it makes you more comfortable, I'm sure we can sort something.'

'It's okay. I'll get used to it.' Callie watched as he went back to the ute, climbed in and started the engine.

Or put a chair against the door.

There were a lot of things she was going to have to get used to. Back with kids, teaching, being with strangers, no working phone, not to mention the isolation.

And this prefab hut was very different to her elegant house in Brisbane.

Even though she'd known she was coming to the outback, she'd not considered the vast distances and the isolation or the rough way she was going to live. It had taken forever to come down that rough road where she'd left her car and had almost lost her luggage. Embarrassment heated her cheeks as she realised how unprepared she was and how stupid she must have looked.

They didn't lock doors and she'd put her luggage in a ditch to keep it safe. Oh well, it would give the girls a laugh when she told them.

With a shrug, Callie headed to the steps as the ute took off in a cloud of red dust. She smiled when Petie waved to her. He was a cute little kid, but she wasn't too sure about the other two. The older one—Rory—had spent a lot of time quietly watching her.

But there was no need to worry about that. As long as she had the parents' support she could handle them. It might have been a while, but she'd dealt with kids with worse behaviour than Nigel when she was at Barfield State School, and his father had reacted appropriately when he'd been rude.

Pulling a face as she walked up the steps to the narrow veranda, she tried to get her responses into teacher mode. After all, that's what she was here for. She was good with kids, and she was usually a good judge of people. Well, she had been once until Greg pulled the wool over her eyes. So she'd be very wary with anyone she met out here. She still hadn't made a call on Braden Cartwright, but her instincts were saying she could trust him.

Keep to herself, not talk about her life or background, while she got herself settled and then decided what she wanted to do with the rest of her life.

Stuff the biological clock. Family and motherhood were no longer an option for her.

Until she'd learned how to be a better judge of people, Callie wasn't going to trust anyone here. Not even the Cartwright family, no matter how kind Braden seemed. He'd probably just been trying to make a good impression saving her luggage; anyone would.

Greg wouldn't have dived into a dirty channel, she thought.

With a shrug, she pushed the door open, and was met by a musty smell overlaid with disinfectant. The donga was basic. One bedroom, a living area with a small television, and a compact kitchenette on one wall. There were two doors at the back. Pushing the first one open she was met by a functional but clean small bathroom and toilet. The other door opened up to a bigger veranda with two plastic chairs and a table. The wind ruffled the water of a small dam not far from the back fence.

Callie stood for a moment looking out over the flat arid land to the west. The sun shimmered in the dust as it headed towards the horizon. There was an eerie quiet and there was no sign of any life. No cattle, no cars, no people. One single tree sat between her donga and the horizon.

And that suited her just fine. Isolation was what she'd wanted, and isolation was what she'd got. Her spirits lifted a little as Callie turned back inside to her new home.

If donga meant small and plain, that's what she was in, but she would cope. It was a bit disconcerting to think this was home for the next who knew how long. It was very different to her beautiful house in the leafy suburb back in Brisbane. That graceful old Queenslander had been her grandparents' house, and they'd left it to her. Dad had always encouraged her to sell it, but she'd hung onto it.

'You can travel, love, and you'll never have any money problems if you invest your cash wisely,' he'd said. 'It needs too much work to hang on to.'

'No, Dad, I love that house. I'll rent it out for the time being, and I'll live there one day when I can afford to do it up.'

She'd never dreamed that day would come so soon. When her parents had been killed in that horrific accident on the Autobahn in Germany Callie had moved out of the family home and sold that. Not being able to handle being there without her parents, she'd put the proceeds of the sale and her inheritance into doing up her grandparents' home, and she'd moved in when it was finished.

Greg had tried over and over to talk her into selling it and invest the proceeds in a share portfolio, but that was the one place she had managed to hold firm. Maybe that was when he had started to lose interest in her—or her potential as a gravy train.

And now thanks to him—or if she was fair— thanks to *her* bad choices, her beautiful home on an acre across the road from the Brisbane River was sitting empty while she was out here in a "donga".

Callie pushed away the negative thoughts as she had a quick shower, and then left the wet suitcase out on the small veranda—there'd be time for that later—and headed across the hard dirt to the main house.

She would be fine.

Chapter 15

Braden settled Rory and Petie in front of the TV with a sandwich and withstood the angry glare from Nigel as he took him to his room after he'd been to the bathroom.

'You can read a book while you eat your sandwich, and then when I've had my shower, we're going to have a chat in the office.'

'Whatever,' Nigel said sullenly.

Braden put the plate with the sandwich on the chair and held his temper as he closed the door. The last thing Nigel needed was temper, and Braden's temper had been on a knife edge since the boys had come home. He loved his sons and he loved having them home—he knew it was where they should be—but he carried so much guilt he worried he wouldn't be enough for them. His anger was at himself for abandoning his boys. Since they had come home—or since Sophie had insisted they come to him—Braden's mind and heart had been forced out of that dark place where he had hidden any feelings for the past two years. He had handled his grief so badly; the boys had suffered more because of his actions.

Before Sophie had taken the boys to their place, and on the too few occasions he'd seen them when she'd brought them back to the station, Braden had known that Nigel was the child who had struggled most with Julia's death.

A surge of fresh guilt rose from his chest as he sat on the side of his bed and dropped his head into his hands, uncaring of the red mud on his trousers. He'd thought that his middle son had improved, and Sophie had told him that Nigel's night terrors had stopped over the past year, but his son's behaviour today told him differently.

Maybe he should have taken the boys to grief counselling like Sophie told him he should.

But he'd thought they were too young.

Shit, he hadn't even gone to the one appointment he'd made in town with the visiting counsellor. Damn it all, he had enough problems dealing with the situation himself. What was the good of talking to someone you didn't even know? Braden carried his own guilt close to his heart and couldn't see the point of sharing it. It wasn't going to bring Julia back.

Nothing would ever bring back his wife and the mother of his children. If he'd known what that day was going to bring he would have stopped her going out to that bloody horse. The first thing Braden had done when he'd come back from the hospital was ring Kent and ask him to take Taffee away.

At least with his boys back home with him he could make sure they were safe. Keep them safe and then work on their happiness—and Nigel's behaviour. Show them how much he loved them and make up for being an absent father.

Braden stood slowly and rubbed his hands over his face before he headed for the shower.

Ten minutes later, scrubbed clean of red mud and without the sour smell of the bore water coming from his hair and skin, Braden headed for the kitchen via the boys' room. Rory and Nigel had twin bunks and Petie's bed was across the big room under the window. They'd chosen the room with the bunks so they could be together. Petie played in there with his toys, but spent most nights in Braden's bed.

Braden had closed up the house at the other side of the breezeway where the master bedroom suite and the boys' old room were. He never went in there. Julia's clothes and possessions were untouched. Strangely the boys hadn't shown any interest in going there either. One day soon he'd tackle it and have a sort out. That was way past time too.

As he walked down the hall Braden frowned and stopped outside the boys' bedroom door. It was closed. Opening the door quietly, he stuck his head in the room.

'Nigel?' He frowned as he looked around; there was no sign of his son. The noise of the television blared down the hall and Braden pursed his lips and headed to the living room.

Disobedient little tyke.

Rory and Petie were sprawled on the floor. But there was no sign of their brother. 'Has Nigel been in here?' he asked.

No response as the blare of the cartoon filled the room.

'Rory!' This time his voice was like a gunshot and he immediately regretted it as Rory jumped and Petie's eyes widened.

'Sorry, guys. Have you seen Nigel?'

Rory stared at him for a moment and then shook his head. 'No, Dad. He's in our room.'

'He might have gone to the bathroom again. How about a Paddle Pop when I come back?' he added by way of an apology.

'Is Nigel in big trouble, Dad?' Rory asked tentatively.

'No, mate. He just needs to learn a few more manners.'

'Maybe you need to give him a clip under the ear when he's naughty.'

Braden froze and stared at Rory. 'I don't think so. You know Mum and I always said that hitting kids to get them to be good was a bad way for parents to behave. And where did you hear that expression anyway?'

Rory put his head down and mumbled. 'Doesn't matter.'

Braden crouched down in front of him. 'It does to me. I don't ever want you to think that I would do or say that.'

'Uncle Jock used to clip Nigel. He told him he was a waste of space.'

'Did he now?'

Rory's eyes glistened with tears. 'I thought you might have changed and might be like Uncle Jock too. I don't want you to get cranky. That's why I've been really good since we came home. Uncle Jock said you didn't want us home, and I'm cranky with Nigel for stuffing it up. You won't send us back there, will you, Dad? If you do I'll be really angry at Nigel for saying "shit" to the teacher lady.'

Braden's heart broke. It was a physical feeling that pressed hard on his chest. He plonked his bum on the floor and held his arms out to Rory. 'Come here, mate.'

He put his arms around his boy, and blinked moisture away from his eyes as Rory's arms crept around his neck.

'Before I go and find Nigel—and no I'm not going to clip him—I want to tell you something very important. I love you guys, and I'm sorry it took so long for me to bring you home. It took me a long time to get over what happened to your mum. I'm really sorry it took me so long. I have a lot to make up to my three special boys. Things are going to change now. We're going to have a teacher for you, and I'm going to get someone to come and help us cook, and someone to help us in the house and garden. And I'll be here as much as I can. I love you three. You guys and Aunty Sophie are my life.'

'Can I start to come out to the cattle with you? I'm eight now.'

Braden ruffled Rory's hair. 'I think that's a good idea.'

'Me too, Daddy?' A little hand tugged at his T-shirt.

'We'll see. Maybe Miss Young will bring you out after your school hours when I'm working the paddocks close to the house. How would that be, Petie?'

'That would be good.'

'Now give me a big hug, both of you, and I'll go and get Nigel.'

'And then our Paddle Pops,' Petie said.

113

'You don't miss a trick, do you, mate?' Braden pushed himself to his feet. 'I'll be back in a minute. Nigel and I just have to have a little bit of a talk.'

Anger seethed through him at the things Rory had said about Jock. He would follow that through later when the boys were in bed.

Braden headed up the hall. The toilet door usually left open was shut. He stood outside and tapped on the door. 'Nige? You okay? You in there, mate?'

There was no reply.

Braden tapped on the door again and when there was no response, he turned the door handle. It was locked.

'Nigel! Unlock the door! Or answer me!' Worry rippled down into his stomach and formed a hard lump.

Braden turned and raced to the kitchen and flung open the second drawer under the counter beside the stove. As he scrabbled through the assortment of bits and pieces—string, bottle tops and sticky tape—in search of the screwdriver he knew was in there, there was a tap at the kitchen door.

'Hello?'

'Yes!' he answered impatiently as his fingers curled around the yellow-handled screwdriver. He looked up as Callie Young pushed the door open. 'Sorry. The boys are in the living room.' Then he realised she didn't know where that was so he hurried over to the door. 'I've got a bit of an emergency.'

'Can I help?'

He almost didn't recognise her because she looked very different to the hot and red-faced woman with the red bandanna wrapped around her head.

Callie Young had showered and damp, dark brown hair hung in ringlets on her shoulders. Fair skinned, delicate shoulders that had been left bare by a strappy sundress. And all the makeup was gone from her face. Her cheeks were flushed a slight pink. He hadn't realised what a pretty girl she was.

Braden immediately killed that thought. 'I've lost Nigel,' he said gruffly. 'I'm worried he's in the toilet and crook. The door's locked from the inside.' He held up the screwdriver. 'Can you keep an eye on the other pair for me. Just follow the sounds of the TV. I said they can have a Paddle Pop. Rory'll show you where they are.'

Before she could answer, he took off back up the hallway.

Chapter 16

Her boss's greeting that he had an emergency and to please sit with the boys and get them a Paddle Pop worried Callie. He had looked distressed as he'd disappeared with a screwdriver in hand.

As instructed, she followed the noise of the television and finally found Rory and Petie ensconced in two small bean bags on the floor of a large room where a DVD was playing at full volume.

'Ah, hello,' she ventured, but wasn't heard.

A second time. 'Hello, boys.'

Finally her loud teacher voice, 'Who wants a Paddle Pop?' gained an instant response.

Two heads flew around to see who was offering Paddle Pops.

Rory's expression was confused, but Petie recognised her straight away. His, 'Yes please, silly Callie,' brought a smile to her face.

She held out her hand. 'Maybe we could turn the TV off for a minute and you can show me where they are?'

Rory picked up the remote and pointed it at the television set like a seasoned pro. 'The Paddle Pops are in the freezer in the laundry.'

'Can you show me where the laundry is?' Callie asked with a smile. 'And then when you have them, maybe you can show me the schoolroom where we'll be doing your lessons.'

Petie took her hand and let her down a hallway followed closely by Rory and two pups. They reached the end of the hall where there was a door in the centre of the house. Petie tried to reach the handle but it was way above his little hand, even though he stood on his tippytoes. Callie leaned over and opened the door, surprised to see a wide concrete breezeway in the middle of the house.

She hadn't realised that the house was virtually split into two and wondered if maybe someone else lived in the other side.

'The freezer's over here,' Rory said. 'We're allowed to have the Paddle Pops out of the top basket.'

The boys led her to a big utility room at the back of the breezeway. Two washing machines, a clothes dryer and two large chest freezers filled the space. Assorted coats and hats hung on a large board on the adjacent wall, plus there was an assortment of boots neatly lined up beneath them. Now that she knew the washing machines were there, she'd sort out her wet clothes later.

A quick glance told her there were only men's boots there. No sign of a woman.

Rory opened the lid of the freezer on the left and pulled out three chocolate Paddle Pops. 'One for you too?' He looked at her cautiously. 'If you want one, that is?'

'No, thank you, but maybe bring that one for Nigel and we can put it in the freezer in the kitchen for when he's ready. I'll have a cuppa with your dad while we talk about my duties.'

'The scissors is in the kitchen,' Petie explained as Callie tried to tear open the shiny wrapping around the frozen treats.

Rory looked at her thoughtfully. 'So you're gonna stay? Even with Nigel being bad?'

Callie tried not to look hesitant. 'Looks like it,' she said. 'I've unpacked, and then I have to get my car fixed in town.'

A couple of minutes later, the two boys were sitting at the kitchen table eating their Paddle Pops and Callie put the third Paddle Pop in the freezer at the top of the large fridge. She was surprised to see it was almost empty. Half a bag of frozen peas sat on the shelf.

'Nigel won't be allowed to have that one,' Petie said as chocolate dribbled down his chin.

Rory shook his head. 'Probably not. He's in trouble with Dad. He's always naughty. Uncle Jock even smacked him a few times and Aunty Sophie got really cranky at him. Not at Nigel, at Uncle Jock, I mean. They had a fight about it.'

Callie raised her eyebrows, unsure of who Uncle Jock and Aunty Sophie were.

'I'm *cwanky* at Nigel too. He's being naughty,' Petie said. 'He's doing it on purpose.'

'Let's have a wash, and go outside and then the puppies can have a run around. Is that okay? Would your dad let you do that?' Callie didn't want to do the wrong thing straight up. She'd already had a bad start with Braden Cartwright.

'Yes, there's a fenced off bit out the back near their kennels. We're allowed out there as long as we look out for snakes.'

'What are their names? The puppies, I mean,' Callie asked as she picked up the facecloth that was hanging over the sink.

'Bumper and Cottie,' Rory replied. 'Nigel has one too. Cottie is the only girl so when they grow up we have to be careful that she doesn't have babies.'

Callie nodded carefully. 'Fair enough.'

'Aunty Sophie gave us our pups when we came home.'

'They're very cute.' Callie said, and wondered who Aunty Sophie was as she wiped Petie's face and hands with the cloth. She had lots of questions but it wasn't the right thing to grill the kids. She'd save them up for the interview with the boss. She turned to wipe Rory's sticky fingers, and looked up as loud footsteps pounded down the timber floor of the hallway from the other end of the house.

Braden came to the door running his hand through his hair, his brow wrinkled in a frown.

'Has anyone seen Nigel? He locked the toilet door and I thought he was in there, but when I got it open, it was his usual party trick of locking the door and shutting it from the outside. I've searched all the rooms and looked under the beds and in the wardrobes, but there's no sign of him.'

Callie shook her head. 'We went out to the laundry, and he wasn't there. We were about to go outside. Should we look out there, or try the other side of the house?'

Braden's voice was terse. 'No, it's all locked up. We don't go in there. Come and help me look outside. He won't be far away.'

But Callie could see the worry etched on his face. She was starting to wonder what the family setup was here. Had she made a big mistake?

Chapter 17

Nigel

Nigel pulled his knees up to his chest and tried to keep as still as he possibly could. Tweedle snuggled into his chest and gave a little huff in his sleep.

He'd done it again. Ruined things for everyone. He thought about running away, but there was nowhere to go. He was too little to go all the way to town, and if Tweedle ran away they could both get lost. Dad would be proud of him for thinking that.

If they lived in a town he could have found somewhere to sleep, he and Tweedle could have found food to eat; it would have been an adventure like those books Aunty Sophie had read to him at night. Someone might have adopted him. He could have had a mummy again, and a daddy who was proud of him.

Nigel blinked as hot tears pushed out of his eyes. He'd stay here for a while and see what happened. At least Dad wouldn't be angry like Uncle Jock was. Dad never hit them.

Another tear squeezed out of his eyes. He didn't want to cry. He hadn't cried when Uncle Jock had got cross, but he'd had Aunty Sophie to cuddle him then.

She didn't smell as nice as Mummy had, but her cuddles had made him feel better.

And now he'd messed everything up again. Aunty Sophie had been their mum for a while but she'd gone all funny when Petie called her Mummy, and then she'd decided to bring them home. Now they were home with their real dad.

Uncle Jock had said, 'About bloody time too.'

Nigel had missed Dad and they had all been excited when Aunty Sophie said they were coming home to their big house. And when they got their puppies, he'd been really happy.

But it was yucky without Mummy here. When he'd cried, Aunty Sophie had told him all about the lovely place where Mummy lived now and that she was watching down on them from up in the sky.

Now he'd gone and opened his big mouth—two times—and the new nanny would leave. He'd hoped that she'd want to stay and be their new mum. But now Dad would have to look after them all the time. But that wasn't too bad, because Dad wasn't as sad anymore. And Dad made the best milkshakes with ice cream.

Another two bloody tears—Nigel bit his lip hard, *don't* say bloody, it's a bad word—rolled down his cheeks and he lifted his fist and rubbed at them.

Tweedle woke up and barked once.

123

'Ssh, go back to sleep.'

Nigel closed his eyes and it wasn't long before he drifted off too, the little pup snuggled up under his chin.

Chapter 18

Callie followed Braden and Rory to the big shed behind the house on the opposite side to the dongas. A couple of small buildings were on the other side of the shed, flanking another long building with a verandah at ground level.

Braden must have noticed her looking around.

'That's more accommodation,' he said, 'but it's empty these days. We use contract stockmen mostly now. The permanent guys live in the original house at the back of the property where the cattle yards are.'

'Is the house fairly new?'

'Yes. My grandparents bought the property back in the nineteen sixties, and moved into the house that was already there. We built the new one.'

We? But she didn't ask.

'Could Nigel have gone to the old house?'

'No, it's about ten kilometres away. There's a back entrance to the property that joins the Charleville road. We don't use it anymore.' He shook his head. 'The road, I mean.'

'How big is the station?' Callie asked. She looked down at her sandals. She should have put boots on; her white sandals were filthy already.

125

Braden pushed open the two wide doors of the machinery shed, and the large space flooded with late afternoon light. If they didn't find Nigel soon, it would be dark. Petie was holding her hand firmly.

'Where do you want us to look?' she asked.

'I'll call him and then we'll look behind the machinery, up in the rafters—there's a couple of ladders—'

'He likes being in the excavator, Dad,' Rory said.

'I know, mate. We'll look in all the machines. You walk around and call Tweedle.' He turned to Callie. 'Watch where you walk here, sometimes there can be snakes in here. They chase the rats that get in the hay.'

'Oh, uh, okay.' She froze and looked down at her bare legs and flimsy—dirty—sandals, but reached down and scooped Petie up off the concrete floor. 'How about I carry you?'

'Yes, please.' The happy look on his face gave her a warm glow, but her chest was still tight with worry.

Worry for the little boy, and worry about what she'd done coming out here. All of a sudden, her problems and life back in Brisbane seemed to disappear; her focus totally on the situation out here. 'Come on, Petie, we'll go over to this side and look in all the nooks and crannies.'

'Nigel, where are you?' She jumped as Braden's voice boomed behind her, followed soon by Rory's equally loud voice calling the dog.

'Tweedle, dinnertime,' he yelled.

The search was fruitless. Half an hour later, they made their way back to the house after searching the machinery shed, the other buildings, and what Braden called the old cookhouse.

'He's gotta be in the house somewhere.' Braden's forehead creased with worry as he pushed open the back gate. 'Rory, you feed the pups and lock them into their run, and we'll go and start doing a room by room search inside.'

'I want to go with Rory and feed Cottie too,' Petie said.

Braden nodded. 'Okay, that would be a help.'

'He wouldn't have gone over to my donga, do you think?' Callie asked as she put the little boy down onto the one patch of green grass. 'I didn't see him on the way over.'

Petie bent down and picked up his puppy, and then followed Rory. 'Bedtime, Cottie.'

Callie looked over at Braden. A pulse was ticking in his cheek.

'Has Nigel ever done this before?' she asked quietly as the boys filled the dog bowls with kibble.

'No. He can be a handful but he's not usually sneaky.' He ran a hand through his hair again

127

making it stick up more. 'I'm sorry the day has ended like this. When we find him, we'll sit down and I'll fill you in. Can you wait out here for the other two and bring them inside when the dogs are settled. If he doesn't turn up soon, I'll ring next door and get some help.'

'Okay.'

Braden turned to the steps and Callie froze as his body tensed and he jerked to a stop. She turned around and followed his gaze. A third puppy had pushed out of the kennels and joined the other two at the food bowls.

'What the hell?' Braden exclaimed as he ran past her to the dog enclosure. Ignoring Rory and Petie and the three pups, he hurried to the last kennel in the row of six—the one that the pup had come from. Callie watched as her employer dropped to his knees and peered through the low arched opening.

'Nigel Cartwright.' His voice was low and calm. 'Found you! Are you going to come inside and have some dinner with us?'

Chapter 19

Callie's throat closed with emotion when she saw the look on Braden's face as he picked Nigel up and rested his head on his son's hair. His eyes glinted with moisture and she held out her hands to the other two boys. There was no sign of the cranky man of this afternoon.

'Come on, you pair. Let's go and get some tea sorted, and your dad and Nigel can lock the dogs in.' She assumed the dogs would be locked in.

'Thank you, Callie.' Braden lifted his head and his voice was husky. 'Nigel and I won't be long.'

The boys took her hand and they crossed the yard together and headed up the back steps into the kitchen. 'What do you usually have for tea?' she asked with a smile, as she wondered what Braden expected of her.

It was a crazy end to a crazy day, but she was sure she could manage to cook something for the boys' tea.

'Pizza?' Rory said hopefully. 'Can you make pizza?'

'Um, depends what's in the fridge,' she said. 'Let's go look.'

'I think Aunty Sophie left some pizzas in the fridge. She's a good pizza maker.'

Callie crossed to the fridge and opened the door of the combined upright fridge-freezer. 'We're in luck!'

As well as some pre-made pizzas there were several casserole dishes full of different meals.

The two boys waited while she took the pizzas from the fridge and put them on the bench. She tipped her head to the side. 'Ah . . . oven or microwave? And how many should I cook? I'm not used to feeding a houseful of men.'

That got a smile from Rory. 'We're not men yet. Daddy's the only man.'

'Silly Callie!' Petie piped up.

'Go and have a wash and I'll put them in one at a time, and then I'll ask Daddy how many when he comes in.'

By the time the microwave dinged three minutes later and the first pizza was cooling on the bench, she'd found the cupboard with plates in it. The table was almost set when the back door opened and Nigel walked in ahead of his father.

'Yum, pizza!'

'The other two have gone to wash their hands,' she said with a quick glance at Braden. His face was set but he did smile when Nigel looked up at him.

'Will I, Dad?'

'Yes. You can go and have a wash and hurry the other pair up. Smells like the pizza's ready. But before you do, don't you have something to do?'

Nigel came over to Callie and looked up at her. 'I'm really, really very sorry I said rude things to you, and I hope you aren't cross at me. And I really mean it—' his squeaky voice sped up '—and I'm not just saying that so you want to stay, because *we* want you to stay. We all do. A lot.'

Callie crouched down in front of the little boy. His eyes were red, and she knew he'd been crying. The look on his face broke her heart and she held out one hand. 'I accept your apology. Thank you, Nigel. I'm looking forward to settling in and getting to know you all.'

Nigel took off and Braden went to the fridge and took out a large container of juice. Callie went back to the cupboard and got out five glasses. They didn't speak.

Well, it looks like I've decided to stay, she thought.

Finally Braden came over to the benchtop where the pizza was cooling and his voice made her jump. 'Thanks, Callie. You were kind to the little demon, and I do appreciate what you've done.'

'It was pretty easy,' she said as he stared at her. Heat filled her cheeks as he kept looking. Finally he

131

turned away and poured juice into each of the glasses.

'Should I put another pizza in the microwave?'

'Thanks, they'll eat the lot. The pizzas have been in the fridge since my sister brought the boys home a few days ago, and they're probably close to their use by date.'

'Aunty Sophie?'

'Yes, my sister, Sophie. She's responsible for all that food in the fridge. We were on our way to town to stock up the pantry when we came across you this afternoon.'

He handed her one of the glasses, and took a swig of his juice. Putting the glass down on the bench, his expression was rueful. 'I could really do with something stronger than this. It's been a day and a half, but we do need to sit and have a chat. The boys can have the pizzas and I'll put one of the casseroles in the big oven and we'll eat after they've gone to bed.' His eyes were dark as he looked over his glass at her. 'Is that alright with you?'

She nodded slowly, but she knew her voice was hesitant. 'We have to talk, and we have to eat, so it makes sense. Can I just ask one thing before the boys come back?'

'Yes?'

'Is it just you and the three boys here?'

'It is. Didn't the job agency fill you in on us?'

'I'm not sure. I might have been a bit stressed when she was telling me about the station and the trip out here.'

The conversation drew to a halt when there was yelling from the hallway and the three boys raced into the kitchen.

Callie lifted the plate with the pizza on it, and put it in the centre of the table, and then slid the second one into the microwave and set the timer. The whole time she was aware of Braden's eyes on her and she felt uncomfortable.

And she didn't even have a car if she had wanted to leave, or a lock on her door to make her feel secure through the night that loomed ahead. Not that she was intimidated by him, or even wary. She sensed he was a good man. A good man in a difficult situation that she hadn't worked out yet.

They were here with no mother or wife and the boys had been away with his sister.

She looked up and encountered his gaze still on her. Lifting her chin with a steadiness she didn't quite feel, she held his gaze. 'While the boys eat, and before we have our chat, could I please use the phone to let my . . . my family know I've arrived safely.'

He didn't need to know she had no family. And she wanted to tell Jen exactly where she was.

'Of course.' Braden finally looked away and gestured to the hall. 'The second door on the right is my study. The phone's on the desk.'

'Thank you.' Callie looked down and hurried out of the room. 'I won't be long.'

'Take your time.'

Chapter 20

By the time the microwave dinged that the third pizza was ready, the first two had been demolished. The boys were quiet as they shovelled ham and pineapple pizza into their mouths and Braden knew he was going to have to do something about their table manners. They'd gone downhill in the months they'd been with Sophie and Jock. But he wasn't going to say anything to them because he knew Nigel was still fragile.

After he and Callie worked out her duties, he'd give Sophie a call. Many of the things that Nigel told him had left Braden uneasy. He didn't like the thought of Sophie being in a relationship with Jock either. He'd never been terribly impressed with him, but he figured Sophie loved him and had seemed happy, so he didn't say anything. He was polite and welcoming to Jock when they visited, but it had been hard work when they'd lived in the donga for a few months.

Sophie had taken up with Jock a few weeks after Julia's accident. He'd arrived to help with the muster, and had flown the helicopter from *Lara Waters*. His mate, Kent, didn't have much time for

Jock but Braden had always put that down to Kent still carrying a torch for Sophie.

'He's got an eye to the main chance, that one,' Kent said one afternoon as they watched Sophie and Jock ride in from the paddocks. 'Just watch him.'

As Braden stood to get some ice cream for the boys, he heard Callie's voice coming from the study, and he smiled when she laughed. She was probably telling her family about leaving her luggage in the irrigation channel.

'Daddy?' Petie's mouth was ringed by red sauce and Braden picked up the paper towel that was in the middle of the table.

'Yes, mate?'

'I like Silly Callie. Aw, don't rub so hard.'

'That's good. I like her too. But maybe she doesn't like being called Silly Callie.'

'I'll ask her,' Petie said importantly.

And Braden did like her, he wasn't just saying that. His first impression had been way off, but she'd been a trooper since they'd got home. Pitched in and helped search for Nigel without a murmur, and hadn't been precious like he'd first expected. He'd been too quick to judge her on the long red nails, the designer clothes, and the expensive luggage. And that sports car.

Despite what Callie had said about dealing with it herself, he'd call Anderson's garage in town tomorrow and get them to come and tow it there at his expense.

Braden served out three bowls of ice cream and then opened the fridge and looked at the neatly labelled containers. With a nod, he pulled out a chicken curry. As he opened the pantry to check if there was rice, Callie came back into the kitchen. Her cheeks were flushed and her hair was mussed as though she'd been running her fingers through it. She had beautiful hair and he wondered if the deep auburn glints under the light were natural.

'Wow, you guys. You must have been hungry,' she said with a grin. Her whole face lit up as she smiled at the boys and Braden found it hard to look away. 'Pizza's all gone and now ice cream!'

'We were,' Rory replied.

Braden was surprised at how quickly the three boys had accepted Callie into the household, and how easy they were with her. It was as though she'd been there for ages, and not just a few short hours. Nigel had apologised for being rude to her, and Petie obviously adored her already. His Sophie love had transferred already. Rory was slower to trust; he was the one most like Braden. He sat back and observed.

If she stayed—and he was hoping now she would—maybe things would be a lot easier.

'Okay, you lot, let's head for the shower, and then Callie and I are going to have a talk about your lessons.'

'Would you like me to do something in here?' she asked.

'I took out a curry and I was about to look for some rice. Does that suit you?'

'Sounds good. You go and deal with the boys and I'll poke around in the kitchen.'

Their eyes met and held and they shared a look of understanding as Nigel stood close to Braden.

'Say goodnight to Ms Young, guys.'

'Callie, please,' she said. 'If that's okay with you. Or Miss Callie.'

'Good night, Silly Callie,' Petie interrupted and they all chuckled.

'Goodnight, Miss Callie,' Rory said shyly, and Nigel repeated the same words.

'Night boys, sleep well. I'll see you in the morning.'

'I won't be long,' Braden said.

Callie was thoughtful as she opened the pantry looking for rice.

Maybe being here was going to be okay.

Chapter 21

'Come on in, Ms Callie. I thought we might make a totally new start.' Braden smiled and held the door of the study open for her.

Callie stepped through in front of him. 'Sounds like a good plan. It's been a strange start.'

She walked over to the desk and he stood and waited for her to sit down before he sat on the other side, the same chair she'd sat in when she'd chatted to Jen. She had shared many of the events of the trip, and the dust storm, with her friend; but about the job, she'd simply told her that she had arrived and the family were good. Jen had her laughing unexpectedly about a phone call from Greg, wanting to know where Callie and *his* car and *his* luggage were.

'Bastard,' Jen had said. 'So I told him you'd flown to Tahiti. He fell for it hook, line and sinker.'

'Oh, Jen. You're a shocker.'

Now Callie turned her attention back to Braden Cartwright as he held his hand out over the desk.

'Good evening, Ms Callie. I'm Braden Cartwright. Welcome to *Kilcoy Station*.'

'Thank you, Mr Cartwright. I'm very pleased to be here.'

139

'Braden, please.'

'Or Mr Braden?' Callie couldn't help saying with a smile.

'Braden is just fine, thank you, Callie.' Her boss leaned back in his chair and his shoulders relaxed. He'd gone in to check on the boys after they'd eaten while she'd loaded the dishwasher. Conversation over their quick dinner had been general, about the weather and the local district and the cattle that he ran on the station. Nothing personal or job wise had been discussed.

'Boys are all asleep?'

'Petie and Nigel are. I let Rory read for a while, but he's under a promise to turn the light out at eight o'clock. He's a good kid. He will.'

'They're all good kids,' Callie said slowly. 'You should be proud of them.'

'I am.' Braden reached up and ran his hand through his hair. She'd already noticed that he did that when he was stressed.

'Shall I tell you a bit about my background, and then you can tell me what you see as my role here?' She thought she'd ease into the conversation.

'I think I need to tell you about our situation first. You may decide it's not for you. I'm sorry the agency woman didn't explain it to you in Brisbane. You might have driven a long way for nothing.'

'So far I like what I see, and being out here, a long way from the city, suits me well,' she said carefully. 'For the time being.'

He nodded slowly and began. 'The three boys have been living with their aunt. My sister.' Braden steepled his fingers in front of him and looked at her. Really looked at her as though waiting for a reaction. As though she should judge him in some way.

She nodded. 'I picked that up. Aunt Sophie.'

And then waited while he stood and turned to a minibar fridge in the corner. 'I'm going to have one drink. Can I offer you one?'

She shrugged. 'Why not?'

'I have white wine or whisky.'

'Whisky on ice if you have ice.'

His eyebrows raised, her response obviously surprising him. 'Coming up.'

A moment later he sat again and placed two glasses with ice and a finger of whisky in each on the table.

He raised his glass and held it up. 'Cheers.'

'Cheers,' she replied, taking a sip as the fiery liquid warmed her throat.

Braden sipped at his and put the glass down. 'My wife and I went to Scotland for our honeymoon, and I discovered fine whisky.' He didn't draw breath and stared at the wall behind her

141

as he continued talking. 'We came back to the station and worked together to build it into a successful concern. We had good seasons and Julia brought a lot of experience from her family cattle station in the Gulf Country. The boys came along, and then Julia was . . . was—' He picked up the glass and drained it.

Callie tensed. She dreaded what was coming.

Braden's voice was flat. 'Julia was killed in an accident. Just over two years ago. I didn't cope. Sophie and her partner took the boys for a while as I dealt with the fallout from the accident. When the coronial investigation was over, I fell in a heap and the boys stayed there. They came back last week and we're making do. I advertised for a nanny and here you are. And before you worry, the finding was accidental death. My wife was crushed by a horse in a storm.'

Coronial investigation? No wonder he had done it so hard. Callie's throat dried and she picked up her glass and sipped until a piece of ice stayed in her mouth. Finally she was able to speak. 'I'm very sorry to hear that.'

'Thank you. I've learned to cope, but I was worried about the boys coming back. I didn't know if I was capable of looking after them. Sophie and her partner decided to move away and she turned up here with the boys and a stack of food last week. Without warning. She figured that was the best way.' He finally looked at her. 'And you know what? I've surprised myself. I guess being a father and loving your kids helps you cope and you know instinctively what to do. It's been easy with them back. The caring part I mean. But not the dealing with their physical needs. Sophie gave me a list of what she said I needed, and I just shot off the nanny request to the agency.' He expelled a breath and she knew how hard it must have been to tell her all that. He sure wasn't holding back, and she appreciated his honesty.

'And you ended up with me. You probably could have done better. I'm just a teacher, but I haven't taught for three years.'

'Callie, so far, your interaction with the boys has been great. They have their problems. Nigel, well, Nigel, you've experienced firsthand. Rory is very wary, and Petie doesn't like to sleep by himself. As far as Rory and Nigel's schooling, Sophie lived closer to town, and they've been going to school in Augathella. It's too far for me to drive them in, so this week they've been home with me while I got sorted. I guess I must have told the agency woman that, and that's how she looked for someone with teaching experience.'

'So tell me what you need.' Callie bit her lip waiting for his response.

Braden did that hand through the hair thing again. 'There's too much for one person. I have to get back out with the cattle as soon as I can—there's a big muster coming up next month. It was Sophie's idea to hire help and she left me a list. You were the first one I asked the agency to fill. Someone for the boys. The rest can fall into place.'

'A list?'

Braden rummaged through the papers on the desk and picked up a piece of A4-sized paper with handwriting on it. He passed it over to her silently.

Callie took it and scanned down the list. 'This many staff would cost you a fortune.' He looked at her strangely and she shook her head. 'Unless you could get one person to do the lot. But this? A fulltime nanny to look after the boys,' she read aloud. 'A housekeeper to keep the house clean, do the washing and ironing. Three days a week. A gardener and a landscaper to keep the yard tidy for them to play in. Someone to drive them to school, and Petie to kindy, unless you find a teacher.' Callie lifted her head and looked at him. 'Well, you've found a teacher.'

'That's one thing ticked off the list, I guess.' He gestured to her glass. 'Would you like another drink?'

'Just a small one with lots of ice and some water, this time please.' A pleasant looseness had filled Callie's limbs and the tension of the day had eased. She was here at the cattle station, and even though it was a bit of a situation here, they were getting sorted and she was hopeful.

And not once in the past hour had she thought of *her* situation or Greg.

Braden rose and came back with their glasses refreshed. 'So, what do you think? Are you interested in taking on the teaching? Living out here? Putting up with us? It's isolated, but we do have some social things with the properties around occasionally if you wanted some entertainment.'

Callie shook her head. 'That's the last thing I want to do. I'm here for peace and quiet.'

He looked at her curiously when she didn't elaborate further. She had enough to think about and wasn't about to complicate matters by sharing her story.

'I'd like to have some time to think about it and then talk to the boys' teachers and see what they're up to. I don't have any doubts that I can take over their lessons, but that doesn't solve the rest of your problems.'

'How about you think about it over the next couple of days? We have to get your car sorted, and we have to go to town to get some groceries.'

'That sounds like a plan. It won't hurt the boys to have some time off. We can catch them up on their work. And I'm sure they need to spend some time with you and settle into being at home again.' Callie put her glass down and stood up. 'Thank you for being so honest with me, Braden. I've got a bit to think about. I'm tired and I'm going to head to bed now.'

'I'll walk you over.' As he stood, the phone on the desk rang.

Callie shook her head. 'I'm fine. You get that. I saw a torch in the laundry. Good night. I'll see you in the morning.'

Braden nodded and turned to the phone as she left the study.

'Soph,' she heard him say. 'I was going to call you later.'

Chapter 22

Braden leaned back in the desk chair. He was happy with the way the day had finally worked out and really hoped that Callie Young would decide to stay.

'Did the nanny arrive?' Sophie's voice dropped in and out as she spoke and Braden could only just hear some of her words.

'Yes, she did. A few dramas getting here, but all's well, I think. We were just winding up a meeting about her duties.'

'And? What's she like?'

Braden took his time answering. 'I think she should work out, if she decides to stay.'

'Why wouldn't she?'

'Ah, let me see, Soph. Maybe because we are hundreds of miles from anywhere. Maybe because I have three boys who have undergone some pretty serious psychological trauma, and maybe because the house is a mess and the pantry is bare. Is that enough to deter a young woman from the city?'

'How young?'

'I don't know, but she graduated her teaching degree about six years ago.'

147

'See that's why you need a housekeeper too. Someone to shop and cook for you.'

'Hang on a minute. I know I need help, but I don't want to fill my house with strangers. If anything happens up there and you ever want to come home you know you're always welcome.'

'What would happen?' his sister snapped back and that was so un-Sophie like, Braden knew straight away there was a problem.

'Are you okay, sis?'

There was a long silence and for a while Braden thought the call had dropped out.

'Wait,' she finally said. 'The service is patchy in here. Hang on, I'll go outside.'

Braden switched the speakerphone on and waited. He could hear Sophie telling Jock she was going outside. He frowned as raised voices came down the line and he heard Jock say 'your bloody family.'

If that guy did anything to hurt his little sister, he would have Braden to deal with. Finally he heard a door closing and then footsteps, and then some scuffling noises before Sophie came back on.

'I'm here again.'

'Where are you?'

The responding giggle was more like his little sister. 'I'm sitting up in a tree near the front gate.'

'Sounds like you. What's the place like?'

'Hot, wet, smelly.'

'Ah, just like home, plus the wet,' Braden quipped. 'Mind you, we were wet here today, but that's a story for when you come home.'

'What makes you think I'll be coming home?' Again the shrewish tone.

'Well, I was hoping that you would come back and visit one day.'

Braden tensed when a strangled sob sounded over the speaker. He bit back the question that was on his lips and waited. The way Sophie was tonight he didn't want to ask questions about Jock.

Finally the waiting paid off.

'I think I've made a mistake, Bray.'

'What sort of mistake, Soph?'

'I don't like it here, and Jock's being . . . being difficult.'

'Come home. And I'm not just saying that because of the boys. I worry about you. I worry that Jock's not right for you.'

'It's not that. He's just unsettled about the change, and he'll calm down.'

'Why would he need to calm down?' Braden decided to say his piece. 'I wasn't happy to hear that he'd been hitting Nigel.'

Another stifled sob.

'Has he hit *you*, Sophie?' Braden's voice was quiet.

'Only once. But it was because he was drunk.'

'I'll give the bastard drunk.'

'I shouldn't have told you. You've got enough to worry about.'

'You're my little sister, and of course I worry about you.'

'It's all good. I'll settle down. He'll settle down. The place is pretty, but it hasn't stopped raining since we unpacked. That's what's making us both moody.'

'Just remember I'm at the end of a phone call. I'll drive up and get you. All you have to do is ask.' Braden clenched his jaw and stared at the window. It was dark outside now, and he hoped that Callie had made her way back to the donga safely.

'I know you would and I love you for it. I'll keep in touch and let you know how I'm doing. I won't make any rash decisions. I'll give it a few weeks. And Bray?'

'Yes.'

'Give those three gorgeous little men a big kiss from Aunty Sophie. And promise you won't worry about me. You've got enough on your plate there. I'm okay. Probably PMT.'

'Too much information. I'll give you a call tomorrow night and let you know what we get sorted here. We're going into town tomorrow to do some shopping, and for Callie to call into the school.'

'Okay. If you need anything, give me a call. Love you, Bray.'

'Love you too, sis. Remember I'm here, won't you?'

'I will.'

Braden put the phone on the desk and walked over to the window. Flurries of dust hung in the faint light cast by the outside lights. It was going to be windy tomorrow according to the forecast, and the cattle were always skittish when it was windy. Not that he'd have time to get out there for a couple of days.

He rubbed his chin and was surprised at how rough it was. He must have looked like a hobo today.

The light was on inside the donga so it looked as though Callie had got back there safely.

Sitting talking to her had been easy, and it had been nice to have a chat and a drink with someone at the end of the day.

Although it mightn't be a good habit to get into. He was worried enough about having more strangers in the house, but Sophie was right. Hiring more help was the only solution if he wanted to keep the boys.

And he would not do anything that jeopardised that.

151

Before he reached the door of the study on his way to check on the boys, his phone trilled again.

'Soph?' he said quickly.

'No mate, it's Kent. I've got some great news. Jon Ingram's back in the district and he's looking for a job.'

'You bloody beauty,' Braden exclaimed. 'I've still got his number. I'll grab him before anyone else does. Thanks for the heads up, mate.'

Chapter 23

Monday

Braden's spirits were high as he backed the ute out of the big shed the following morning. Petie had slept in his own bed all night, the boys had been well behaved at breakfast and hadn't complained that they were out of cereal.

Jon Ingram had called him straight back and agreed to come and work for at least six months. The load that news took off Braden's shoulders contributed to his good mood and he grinned.

Nigel had gone out to feed the dogs without a complaint, and came back in whistling. When Callie Young had appeared at the back door as they were loading the dishwasher, Braden had been startled by the thump his heart gave when she'd walked into the kitchen, and he frowned now as he brought the ute around.

Don't know where that came from, he thought. And it wouldn't be doing it again. It was just his good mood and the novelty of seeing a woman. The blue skirt and colourful top were bright and cheery, and Callie's hair was pulled back from her face in a braid. The shadows had left her eyes and she looked fresh and attractive.

153

Petie was on one side holding her hand, and Nigel on the other. Rory was looking grown up with his hair slicked back, and standing a little way off to the side. He and Nigel were excited about going back to school to see their friends, and Braden had agreed if it was all right with their teacher they could stay at school while he did the groceries and went to the produce store, and Callie spoke to the their teachers. He'd called Kimberley Riordan—the deputy principal and long-time friend—at home to make an appointment for Callie.

'Come in any time, Braden. I'm off face-to-face teaching this morning, and I can fit her in whenever you get here. How are the boys?'

'They're good. Excited to have a nanny.'

'I'll look forward to chatting to her.'

Braden had smiled to himself. If Callie wasn't up to scratch, Kimberley would tell him.

Callie smiled at him tentatively as she stood in the doorway flanked by his sons. She looked like a teacher today, and her appearance was hard to reconcile with the woman striding away from her broken down sports car.

The trip into town was quiet. Callie took a great interest in the landscape, but he suspected it was so they didn't have to make small talk. Plus he'd been a bit brusque yesterday, but he thought he'd cleared the air last night.

A couple of times he went to speak to her but the first time, Nigel interrupted, and the second time she was intent on the view.

A harsh and rugged view that he knew every inch of, but the sky was clear again today and the light didn't seem as harsh as usual. The distant mountains had a misty blue glow and the irrigated paddocks beneath provided a rare green patch in the arid red dirt.

Fifteen minutes into the trip, they approached the section of the road where she'd left her car. As they approached, Callie stared ahead, and sat up straight and then turned to Braden.

'Isn't this where my car was?'

'It is. But the garage has already been out and put it on a truck and taken it back into town. I called them first thing. Old Jim Anderson opens up at seven.'

'Thank you,' she said quietly. 'I appreciate it.'

'Just have to wait and see what he says about it. Looked like a wheel bearing to me. Those low sports cars aren't built for our roads.'

'I know.' She pulled a rueful face. 'Something else I've learned. We city slickers are pretty naïve about the outback.'

'When it gets fixed, it might be better to leave it in storage in town. You can use Sophie's Camry wagon. She left it for whoever came out here to use. There's a seat in it for Petie too.'

'I'll see what they say at the school.'

So far, Callie hadn't given him any indication of whether she'd accept the job, and a little ripple of worry settled in his gut.

Hopefully by the time the day was over he'd have an answer. He really hoped it was a yes.

***

'Are you registered with QCT?' the deputy principal asked Callie after they had discussed the boys' progress.

'Yes, I have full registration.'

'And from what I understand, Braden doesn't have time to drive them into town to attend school.'

'That's correct. I believe that when his sister had the boys, she lived close to town and drove them in each day.'

'She did.' Kimberley sat back in the chair and picked up a pen and tapped it on the desk. 'Braden has given permission for me to share the boys' history and files with you.'

Both Nigel and Rory were achieving to the standard required, but Kimberley Riordan, the deputy, had concerns about them being taught at home. 'I'll be direct, Callie. I'm sure you're a suitable teacher, but the boys need to be at school.

They need the contact with other children, they need to socialise and experience a normal school day. They've both had sessions with the school counsellor on various occasions over the past year, and Nigel in particular is carrying some unresolved issues.'

'I don't think the grief of losing a mother is ever resolved at any age, do you?' Although as a teacher, Callie could see the deputy's point and she understood where she was coming from.

'Of course it's not.' Kimberley looked at Callie and moisture sheened her eyes. 'Callie, we're a small town and a tight community. The circumstances of Julia's death were awful.' She removed a tissue from the box on the desk and dabbed at her eyes. 'As well as me going to school with Braden, Julia was my best friend, and I've known the two oldest boys since they were born. So as well as a professional interest, I also have a personal interest in seeing what's best for them. Nigel has been in my class this year, and I've seen his behaviour worsen as the terms passed.'

'Yes, in the two days since I arrived, I've seen some issues arise. He's a little boy who is hurting. I totally understand your concerns, and to allay them please know I've had a lot of experience with troubled children. Not recently, but in my three

157

years at my school. If it reassures you, I'll send you a copy of my school references.'

'So you left the system and you've been working as a governess for a while?'

Callie had been so intent on listening to Kimberley and trying to find the best solution for the boys she'd forgotten all about her fear of being recognised. Guilt tugged at her. In the scheme of things, her worry was about a superficial situation. There were two little boys here, whose education— and happiness—depended on her honesty.

She drew a deep breath. 'No. This is the first position I applied for.'

'But you've been in education?'

'No.' Callie lifted her head and looked directly at Kimberley. 'I was working for a television network in Brisbane.' She waited for any recognition, but there appeared to be none. She swallowed. 'I'll be honest with you, Kimberley.'

'Please.'

'Leaving teaching was a wrong move. I wasn't in a good place. I'd just lost my parents—'

'You understand loss,' Kimberley said quietly.

'I do. Then I made some errors of judgment in a relationship, and in my career, and a recent event led to me quitting my job at the network, and thinking about my future and what I really want.' She shrugged and stared down at her hands, surprised to see them curled tightly in her lap. She forced herself to take a breath and relax. 'What I'd wanted was to get married and have a family, but that didn't work out. So all my energy now is going back into teaching. Let's just say I knew it was going to be easier out of the city. I applied for the job with the Cartwrights—not knowing the situation—but now that I do, I'm prepared to stay. I just wanted to see the boys' progress, before I made a final decision. I haven't told Braden yet.'

'Callie? I've got an idea. Give me ten minutes.' Kimberley gestured to the coffee machine on a round table near the office window. 'Make yourself a coffee and keep an open mind. I won't be too long.'

Callie nodded and walked over to the table and chose a coffee pod from the selection. Soon the aroma of brewing coffee filled the small office. Standing at the window, she looked out over the playground and smiled. It was morning break time and she could see Rory and Nigel playing handball. Kimberley was right; they needed to be at school but they lived too far out of town to be driven in every day.

Or did they?

But the problem was if she offered to drive them in, and they attended school she'd be out of a job. With a frown, she bit her lip.

159

Unless she agreed to take on one of the other positions that Braden's sister had listed. She didn't mind cooking, and once the house was tidied up, it wouldn't be hard to keep clean.

Her phone beeped in her pocket. She had given Braden her number so she knew when he was ready to pick them up.

I've been delayed at the rural produce store. Will be another hour. Sorry. We'll have lunch in town. That should keep Nigel happy □ Braden.

She quickly typed a reply. **No prob. Still in meeting with Kimberley. I have coffee □**

Callie waited at the window sipping her coffee as she watched the playground activities. Two teachers stood chatting as they did playground duty, and a group of girls with a skipping rope were counting out at the top of their voices. She felt more at home in this unfamiliar school than she ever had at Channel Eight. She'd missed the school environment; it was her happy place. Once she went back to Brisbane—eventually—she'd find a school close to home and settle back into teaching.

The door opened and Kimberley came back in followed by a young guy in a suit.

'Callie, this is Bob Hamblin, our principal.'

Bob held his hand out and Callie took it. 'Welcome to Augathella, Callie. Kimberley asked me to come in and meet you because she's had an idea that I see has merit.'

Kimberley looked intently at Callie. 'I didn't want to suggest this to you before I ran it by Bob, but he agrees that it's a good idea. I hope you do too.'

'I think I know what you're going to say and I agree. I was going to ask Braden what he thought about me driving the boys in every day, and taking on more of a nanny role at the house.'

Kimberley's smile was wide. 'You've got it half right, but what we'd like to do is offer you a casual teaching position. As you probably know, we have a shortage of teachers out here. All the new graduates want the coast or the city, and here you are dropped in our lap so to speak.'

Bob took over. 'We thought three days a week would suit both ways. You could drive the boys in, work at the school and then drive them home and then teach them at home on Thursdays and Fridays. I know it'll depend on your employer, plus you agreeing, but it would be good for the boys.'

'Also, Petie has been going to preschool three days a week and he could do that on the days that you teach. The kindy is affiliated with the school,' Kimberley added.

Callie didn't know what to say. Finally she found her voice. 'Wow. What can I say? It sounds like the ideal solution to me, but it's up to the boys' father.'

Kimberley reached over and put a hand on Callie's arm. 'I thought it might be easier for you if I spoke to Braden. After all, how long have you been here?'

'Um, not very long.'

Chapter 24

Three weeks later

'Bags, dogs, chooks, and wash,' Callie called as the boys tumbled from the Camry station wagon on Wednesday afternoon three weeks later. Braden had agreed and thought the school idea was great. The boys were happy to stay with their friends, and Callie had been at the school for three weeks and had settled into the school environment from the minute she walked in. She'd been given a Year Six class, and she wasn't teaching Rory or Nigel, but they still gained some street cred from their "nanny" being a teacher at their school.

'I'll do the dogs,' Rory called as Callie went around to the back seat and got Petie out of the booster seat.

'Aw, I don't want to feed the chooks,' Nigel whined. 'You always get to let the dogs out. Not fair.'

One look from Callie was enough to get him moving towards the chook pens.

'I'll go and get your afternoon tea on the table,' she called after them. 'Don't forget to have a really good wash in the laundry.'

'And change our school clothes,' Nigel called over his shoulder with a grin. 'And I bags feeding Bluey.'

'Can we have Milo, please, Mu …Silly Callie?' Petie asked as she swung him down to the ground.

'If you carry your bag inside,' she replied. Petie was the cutest and best behaved of the three of them, but she'd had to talk to him about him trying to call her Mummy. So far the talk had worked.

The past three weeks had been so good. The only flaw had been the disagreement with Braden about her salary. She'd told him that he was not to pay her for the three days she was teaching and he had insisted that he would.

'You can use that to hire a cleaner.'

'You're still looking after the boys on those days. You're driving in and out of town, and I'm going to pay you.'

If she'd told him that she hadn't taken the job for the money, he probably wouldn't have believed her. Callie had never got around to telling anyone here the real reason she'd left Brisbane, just that general first chat with Kimberley about wanting to get away. No one seemed to have recognised her, and her embarrassment had eased a lot.

But she still didn't want Braden to know about it. His opinion mattered to her, and she didn't want him to think less of her. The first impression she'd made had been bad enough, but she felt as though she'd redeemed herself a bit now.

It didn't really matter anymore. A flash in the pan, and surely something else would have taken over social media by now.

Maybe her reaction had been extreme—fleeing almost a thousand kilometres across the outback—but Callie was pleased she had. She was very happy with the way things had worked out.

There was only one thing that was unsettling her. Why did Braden's opinion of her matter so much?

She told herself it was because she wanted to be a good employee. It had nothing to do with the strong attraction that simmered every time she was with him. A couple of times their eyes had met and held and she had forced herself to look away.

Quickly.

That's how she had first noticed Greg. The eye contact and the long stares. And look where that had got her.

Callie shook herself from her thoughts as the back screen door slammed. 'Milo's ready,' she called.

Five minutes later, the three boys were sitting at the table eating everything she put in front of them.

'Then homework,' she said to Rory and Nigel. 'Petie, you can tell me what you learned at kindy today. You can all sit here at the kitchen table while I peel the vegetables for dinner.'

'Sh—I mean sugar, I forgot Bluey.' Nigel slid off his chair as the clatter of hooves came from the breezeway.

'Can you mix up the Denkavit by yourself?' Callie felt very knowledgeable knowing what a calf needed to drink.

'Yeah, Dad cut a two litre plastic container in half for me so I can fill the other one easier.'

'Okay, well don't be long, you've still got homework.'

Callie had never had much to do with animals but the red baby calf was the cutest little thing. The boys were hand feeding him, but the calf had taken a liking to Nigel.

Callie was cooking the evening meals and the household had settled into a routine. When she'd accepted the position at the school, she and Braden had sat down and worked out a schedule and her duties, and a salary that she had disagreed with.

'We'll see how this goes and then talk about it,' she'd said to Braden last night after the boys were in bed. Watching the way he listened to them, and interacted with them—his love and displays of affection—was heart-warming. He supervised their baths and teeth cleaning every night and then spent half an hour with the boys reading and talking. She wondered if he was trying to make up for the lost time they'd been away with their aunt and uncle. It didn't matter if the phone rang for him, or a worker came to the door, he would stay with the boys during that time. Callie had been surprised at the number of visitors over the past couple of weeks; the station wasn't as quiet as she'd first thought.

The callers were always to do with the cattle and the upcoming muster. Some were happy to leave a message, some waited the half hour until he was free.

She'd also added, 'If you only pay me for half the week, you can afford to get someone out to clean for that half the week and maybe do the yard.'

'I don't expect you to clean the house.'

'I know you don't, but your sister's right. You do need to get someone.'

'Okay, I'll work on it tomorrow.' Braden had put his head back and closed his eyes. They were sitting out on the veranda before she went back to her donga—that was part of the routine, and she'd catch him up with how the boys were doing at school.

The boys did their homework and Callie had cooked dinner by the time Braden came in and showered. Tonight she had no lessons to prepare so she was going to go back to the donga and send some emails. Braden had hooked her laptop up to the satellite network the first week she started at

167

school, and she knew it was well past time to touch base with Jen again.

Chapter 25

As Callie was clearing the table and Braden was bathing the boys, a white ute came around the driveway and parked at the back of the house. She wiped her hands and went to the back door to greet the visitor.

A tall rangy guy carrying a small esky walked across from the ute and grinned at her as she stepped out onto the back veranda.

'G'day,' he said taking his Akubra off. 'You must be Callie. I'm Kent from next door.'

'Hello,' she replied closing the door behind her. 'Braden's just bathing the boys and then he'll read to them for a while. He'll probably be half an hour or so. Can I get you a cuppa or a drink?'

'I brought a six pack for Braden and I.' Kent held up the small esky and then headed for the outside table. 'Sit down with me and tell me about yourself while we wait for him. I've heard good reports from the school.'

Callie glanced into the kitchen and then shrugged. She was almost done in there. 'Okay, I'll just grab a soft drink.'

When she came back out with a glass of Coke and ice cubes, Kent had uncapped a beer and was looking out to the low mountain range to the west. The sky was a pale apricot and the low clouds were tinged with sunset gold. Callie sat on the chair opposite Kent, hoping that Braden wouldn't mind her socialising. 'Do you have kids at the school?' she asked.

'Hell no, I'm a confirmed bachelor,' was the laconic reply. 'My sister works there. Jacinta. Have you met her?'

'I have. She teaches kindy. Does she live out here too? I haven't had much time to chat to anyone yet.'

'No. She lives in town. She's got a year's contract at our school and then at Christmas she's heading north to Cairns. Her boyfriend works on the tugs in the harbour.'

'Did you grow up here?'

'We did.' He chuckled. 'And Jacinta's busting to get away. She'll soon learn there's no place like home. So a teacher, hey?' Kent lifted the bottle and drank deeply.

'Yep. And I love it.'

'And what about being out west? What do you think of our region?'

'It has its own beauty,' she said. Lifting her glass Callie pointed to the sunset. 'Look at that.'

The back door opened and Braden appeared.

'Hey, Kent. I was hoping you'd swing by. I want to run an idea by you.'

Callie stood and picked up her glass. 'I'll leave you two to chat.'

Braden put his hand out and touched Callie's arm. 'Please stay, Callie. No need to go. Kent and I will just talk work if you go. We'd appreciate your company.'

She hesitated for a few seconds and then sat back down on the chair she'd vacated.

***

Braden stayed standing. 'Can I top up your Coke?'

'Thank you. Just a quarter hour and then I've got work to do.'

Braden hurried to the kitchen and put fresh ice in her glass before he topped it up. The boys had gone straight to sleep. Three days back at school and kindy had worn them out. Petie had gone to sleep before he even started reading and he was pleased when the older two nodded off after fifteen minutes. It was usually "one more glass of water", or "one more story, please Dad" and bedtime could drag out.

But he loved it. Having the boys home was great. He should have woken up to himself and brought them home months ago.

Them going to sleep quickly tonight had suited him. He'd been anxious to get out onto the veranda with Callie before she went over to her donga. He told himself he was keen to sort out her salary and talk about the best days to get a cleaner in, and what those duties would be, but deep down Braden knew he just wanted to spend more time in Callie's company.

He hadn't heard a car or her talking to someone until he came back into the kitchen. Kent was sitting across the table from her and watching her as she spoke to him. The feeling that hit Braden was unfamiliar. Callie was wearing the dress she'd worn to school today, and her hair was still pulled back in a ponytail, showing off her pretty face and high cheekbones. The red nails and the red lipstick had gone, and he felt as though the real Callie had emerged. He didn't know what made her tick and why she had come out west, but he knew he was spending way too much time thinking about her.

The feeling that surged through him when he saw her talking to Kent wasn't exactly jealousy, but it was an unfamiliar feeling and he put it aside to examine later.

He sat on the chair on the other side of Callie and the conversation turned to the upcoming muster.

'Have you ever seen a helicopter muster, Callie?' Kent asked.

Her attractive laugh tinkled in the evening air. 'Kent, I've never been out of the suburbs of Brisbane so that would be a definite no.'

'Have you got a new pilot yet?' Braden asked. He couldn't believe Jock's timing in leaving the district. He would have known how hard it would be to get a replacement pilot. He wondered if Jock had deliberately chosen the time, and Kent's comments echoed his thoughts.

'Don't get me bloody started on Jock Evans.' Kent flicked an apologetic glance to Callie. 'Sorry, Callie.'

She lifted one hand. 'It's fine. I'm enjoying the quiet of the evening. I'm the extra here, don't let me stop you talking about work. I'm sure that's why you're here.'

Braden chuckled. 'Kent and I have been doing this for a long time , and we've solved many of the problems of the world on this veranda.'

Not to mention a few huge nights when they had both gotten rip roaring drunk after Julia's accident. Kent had been a mainstay for him. He was a good mate and Braden was still pissed off that Sophie had dumped him.

Callie sat there quietly as Kent quizzed Braden about the extra staff they'd hire between the two properties next week.

Kent reached for a third beer. 'I'm stoked that Jon Ingram is keen to come back here.'

'You and me both, mate,' Braden said, putting his empty bottle on the table. One beer would do

173

him. He kept his ears open for the boys through the night. 'If he's keen on hanging around, I'll even give him a managerial role.'

Callie finally contributed with a cheeky smile. 'Can this guy clean houses and weed gardens?'

Kent rolled his eyes. 'Probably, he's a champion at everything he does and a really nice guy to boot.'

Braden nodded. 'He's a great cattleman and we're lucky Jon's decided to come back to our area.' He pulled a face when Kent winked at Callie.

'You'd better watch out though, Callie. Jon's a ladies' man through and through. He leaves a trail of broken hearts wherever he goes. After the last B&S ball there was even a cat fight over him at the bush breakfast,' Kent warned.

'No fear of that with me,' Callie replied as she stared over the veranda railing and focused on the sunset.

Braden wondered what had made her so independent. He had noticed she was averse to being told what to do, even if she came around and did it in the end. Someone had done a number on her and he wondered if that was why she had fled from Brisbane to a job she knew nothing about before she arrived.

Maybe one day when he earned her trust, he'd ask her why.

Or maybe not. It was none of his business, he told himself. Callie was an employee. Nothing more, and she was entitled to her privacy.

'Earth to Braden. You can't go to sleep after one beer, mate. You're losing your man status.'

'What?' He looked at Kent who was shaking his head.

'I asked you what you thought about old man Anderson's son's latest.'

'What's Billy doing this time?'

Poor Jim Anderson had hoped his son would take over the garage one day but Billy Anderson had never been interested. He flitted in and out of town every few months, always with a different scheme going.

'He's bought the produce store.'

'Fair dinkum!'

'And the bakery and the IGA store, so the grapevine says. We've missed you at the pub the past few weeks and you've missed all the local goss.'

'Where did he get the money for that?' Braden asked.

'Story is he won the lottery. But I'm not so sure about it.'

'He's always been a shonky one. A bit of a worry to know that he's running those businesses. The town depends on them. If it's true.'

175

'Apparently it is, but he's put managers in, Jeff at the pub said.'

'And Jeff would know.' Braden and Kent clinked bottles and chuckled.

'I have been out of the loop,' Braden said. 'We've been pretty busy here since the boys came home, haven't we, Callie?' He looked across the table and was surprised to find her eyes on him. Her cheeks went pink and she looked away.

'Don't let him make you work too hard,' Kent said with a wide smile at Callie. 'You're not on duty twenty-four seven. You can leave the station.'

'I'm happy with the way things are. I'm a bit of a loner, I don't need to go out.'

'We'll see about that. At the end of the muster we have a big bush dance. You'll have to come to that.'

'It's a long time since I've been to one of them,' Braden said.

Kent's smile faded and his voice was gentle. 'Might be time to get back out in the real world, mate.'

'Could be.' Braden kept his tone noncommittal. He knew well that Kent could be like a dog with a bone. He glanced at Callie as the legs of her chair scraped on the timber boards.

'I'm going to leave you guys to chat. I've got some work to do tonight.'

'Don't work too hard,' Braden said. 'You've been looking after us so well, plus you've been working two jobs for three weeks. Maybe you could take a day off tomorrow.'

Callie's eyes widened and she put her hands on her hips. 'No way. The boys will have lessons tomorrow and Friday, and then if we get everything done early on Saturday I might think about taking some time off then.'

Braden had been told off—again. 'Rightio. We'll go for a drive around the property and we'll show you all the sights. We'll take a picnic. The boys would like that. There's a swimming hole over near the mountains. How would you like that?'

'We'll see what Saturday brings,' Callie said. 'Goodnight, Kent. It was a pleasure to meet you. Good night, Braden. I might not see you in the morning, but I'll get the boys' breakfast and we'll be in the school room by eight o'clock so we can finish by two.'

He moved his chair back as Callie waited to move past him.

As she walked in front of him, he reached out and lightly touched her hand, ignoring the spark that ran up his arm. 'Goodnight, Callie, and thank you.'

She walked down the steps and headed for her donga. Braden stared after her until she had disappeared in the darkness.

Kent put his beer bottle on the table. 'What's going on there, mate?'

'What do you mean?'

'I haven't seen you look at a woman like that for a long time.'

'Don't be stupid. Callie's an employee. I'm just trying to make her welcome.'

It was hard to see Kent's expression in the dark. 'Be careful, Braden. You don't know her. Seems strange she turned up out of the blue from Brisbane. Why would someone like her come out here?'

'She answered my ad.'

'Whatever you say. But be careful. Don't leave yourself open, and for God's sake, don't look at her with those big cow eyes when there's other people around. You'll be the talk of the district.'

Braden reached up and flicked the light on as he glared at Kent. 'I think you've had too much to drink, mate. You're dreaming.'

'Am I? Do you know what she did before she came out here?'

'She was a teacher.'

'Maybe she was, but for the past few years she's been a television personality.'

'Bullshit.'

'No, it's true. Jacinta recognised her, but no one at school has told her that it's common knowledge now, because apparently she went through a tough time. Her bloke made a fool of her on television.'

'Her bloke?' Braden's hand stilled as he went to lift the beer bottle to his lips.

'Yeah, apparently they were engaged and he did the dirty on her. So she hasn't been honest with you. Be careful, mate.'

***

Callie lay in the single bed in the donga and watched the fan going round and round like her thoughts. Kent was a nice guy, but she'd had to force herself to pay attention to what he was saying a lot of the time. She had been too aware of Braden near to her and when he'd touched her hand when she was leaving, she'd jumped. She'd been on *Kilcoy Station* for less than a month and she'd been pulled head first into this family. She didn't know what to do.

The crazy thing was that she loved being out here. She loved teaching at the school, she was getting to know the parents and the community, and she loved living at the station.

Well, maybe not so much being in the donga—it was very different to her beautiful house—but she only slept and showered here; she spent most of the days and evenings in the house. And therein lay her dilemma.

She was getting too involved with the family, and too quickly. She loved the boys, she loved the house, she loved the work and she loved . . . no, it was just that her heart went out to Braden. Sometimes he looked so sad, she just wanted to put her arms around him and hold him and comfort him.

His grief and the boys' issues made her silly *#wrongforecast* experience and Greg seem so superficial. The three years she'd spent at the network had been a stupid choice; she should never have left teaching.

Callie rolled over and thumped the pillow. Her heart was telling her to stay and deal with the issues here. Not to run away again.

Logic told her to leave now, because her heart was getting way too involved on too many levels.

It was a long time before she went to sleep.

Chapter 26

Despite a restless night, and crazy dreams, Callie was up bright and early the next morning, but she waited until she heard Braden's ute leave before she headed over to the house. The boys would be fine; Braden would have checked on them before he left and he knew she was always over there before seven-thirty. Often she'd go over before Braden left, and have a cuppa with him, but this past week, she'd been trying to spend less time alone with him. They had their routine down pat, and the boys' well-being was the top priority for both of them.

Callie filled in an hour before Braden headed out, writing an email to Jen to reassure her, and tell her how much she was enjoying her time in the outback.

Getting the job at the school was a fabulous outcome, she wrote. *Best of both worlds. Braden is really happy with the arrangement and it's good for the boys and good for me. Braden is going to hire a house cleaner to come in on those days. He suggested that he gets someone who can do some cooking on those days to stock the fridge so I don't have to cook.*

He's a great employer.

It's really different out here, Jen. But beautiful. The sunsets are spectacular and my donga (don't you love that word) and the house and school are air conditioned so it's easy to put up with the heat.

My car is still getting repaired, but I am driving Braden's sister's car. She's the one who had the boys for two years. Braden's taking care of getting my car repaired.

I met his mate, Kent, last night. He came over to have drinks with us on the veranda. He owns the property next door. I've made some friends at the school. They are all young teachers. I think Bob, the principal, is under thirty!

Braden says…'

Callie bit her lip and read over what she'd typed. Braden this and Braden that. It was like when she and Jen were teenagers and all they wanted to do was talk about the current guy they were interested in. That worried her; she knew she spent way too much time thinking about Braden. She really liked him, and knew that she had to stop herself getting in any deeper. She reminded herself of what had happened with Greg. She wasn't ever going to trust a man again. But she knew Braden was different; he was a good man and she knew she could trust him. It was only because they were in close quarters that she was thinking about him so much.

And how did that explain the faster heart beat when she saw the ute come home, or when she turned into the gates of the property?

She hit the delete key and removed all, except one, mention of Braden.

Hope all is well there. Give the kids a kiss from me. Talk soon. Miss you heaps, Love Callie.

Pressing send, she logged out and snapped her laptop closed. She wouldn't need it over at the house because there was a computer set up for the boys to use in the schoolroom. As she made her way over to the main house, she could see the dust hanging over the road where the ute had driven out. Braden was heading away from town, and she guessed he was going over to Kent's place as they'd discussed last night.

Braden had given her the number of the sat phone so she could call him in case of any emergency, but she'd never had to use it.

Humming beneath her breath, she made her way across to the house.

All was quiet. Flicking the kettle on for a second cup of coffee, she took out three bowls as well as the packet of Weetbix, and checked the toaster was on.

The boys were good sleepers and the three days they drove into town, Callie always made sure she came across to the house earlier to wake them up so they'd have plenty of time for the drive into Augathella. It didn't matter so much on Thursdays and Fridays when they worked from home, but she still liked to keep to a routine.

The kettle flicked off and Callie reached for the instant coffee, and put two slices of bread in the toaster before she headed up the hall to the boys' room. As she was walking up the hall, she heard a muffled noise coming from the family room where the boys watched their DVD movies. As she stood at the door, her eyes settled on the large television screen.

How could she have let herself get so stressed by what happened at the network? With hindsight, she now knew that Greg had done her a huge favour. As she turned away from the door, another muffled noise came from the sofa in front of the TV. With a frown she walked quietly into the room and looked over the back of the sofa.

Nigel was curled up at the far end hugging a pillow, his little cheeks flushed and his nose red.

'Oh sweetheart, are you sick?'

As Callie hurried around the sofa, Nigel gave a great shuddering sigh and she realised he was crying. Without thinking, she sat beside him and held her arms open. She'd been careful with hugs and cuddles over the past weeks, staying as distant as she could; not wanting the boys to get too dependent on her for affection.

Nigel shook his head and turned his head away from her. 'No. Not sick.'

'Did you see your dad this morning?' Maybe he'd got into trouble, but Callie couldn't imagine Braden leaving with Nigel so upset.

'No.' Another sniff. 'But I fed Bluey after he left and then I came in here.'

'Did Bluey stamp on your foot again.'

'No.' Nigel nestled into her, and she placed a hand on his forehead to check he wasn't running a fever.

'What's wrong then, sweetie?' Did you have a bad dream?'

Two little hands crept around her waist and Nigel rested his head on her shoulder. 'No. Rory made me cry.'

'Do I need to speak to him?'

'No! Don't listen to him. It might give you the idea.'

'The idea?' Callie frowned as Nigel began to cry again. His hands held onto her T-shirt, bunching the cotton in his fists. 'What idea, Nigel?'

'Rory said you're not going to be our new mummy. That you're only our teacher. Forever and ever.' He lifted his head back and sniffed. 'I told him he was wrong because I have Mrs Riordan at school and Rory has Mr McIntyre. They're our teachers. Not you. You were here first before you went to school to help the other kids. So you're ours. I told Rory you're here to be our new mummy and he laughed and told me I was a big sook. He said that when it's school holidays you'll probably leave and we won't have you after Christmas. And he said'—another sniff—'we have to be big boys then and look after ourselves because Daddy has to go out and work with the cattle.' Nigel's chest heaved in another shuddering sigh. 'Mummy went away, and then Aunty Sophie left us here, and now Rory said you'll leave too. What's wrong with me, Callie? Is it because I'm the naughty one?'

'Oh, sweetie. No, of course not. You've been so good. At school and at home. And your school work is excellent.'

'So why will you leave us? Why can't you be our new mummy? I'm the only boy in Year One without a mummy.'

Callie's heart broke and she held him close rubbing his back through his PJs as she tried to think of the right thing to say. She was going to have to talk this out with Braden. She doubted if he knew how deep Nigel's issues were.

'I'm your nanny, and your teacher on the days we're not at school, Nigel. One day I probably will go back to my house in Brisbane. I live on a big wide river and I have lots of trees for treehouses and making swings. When I live back there, and you're a bit older, you could all come and visit me.'

'But why can't you be our mummy? You like it here, don't you?''

'I do.'

'So I don't get it. You like Daddy, don't you?'

I do, Callie thought. *Way too much.*

'I do. And your daddy is my employer.' She kept her voice brisk. 'And I like the three of you very much, and I love being your teacher here, and I love being your nanny and helping Daddy look after you. I love *Kilcoy Station*, and I love your puppies. So I think I'll be here for quite a while yet, so you can stop worrying. One day, you might have another mummy, but what you have to remember is that your daddy loves you very much.'

'Will you promise not to leave without telling us? Mummy did and she was yelling at Daddy before she left.'

Callie kept her face blank as her heart broke for the burden Nigel was carrying.

'When it's time for me to leave one day, I *promise* I'll tell you all with plenty of notice. We'll even have a party with cake and—'

'Coke?' Nigel said hopefully.

Callie ruffled his hair. 'We could maybe even have Coke just once.'

Nigel sat up and smiled at her. 'I really hope you keep *all* your promises.

Chapter 27

It was a difficult day in the schoolroom. The two older boys had been impossible to keep on task, and Petie had refused to leave the room and had been clingy. Despite the air conditioning, the heat had built all day, and a headache formed behind Callie's temples. She'd been worrying about Nigel and his insistence on her being their new mummy. She knew no matter how much she loved the job, and the family, she would have to set strict guidelines for her continued stay. Her presence would contribute to Nigel's hopes.

And hers. She forced that thought away.

At two o'clock, Callie wiped the perspiration from the back of her neck and called end of day. 'Let's have an early mark, guys. And maybe a swim?'

Braden had filled the pool a couple of weeks ago and Callie had been pleased to see that all three boys were strong swimmers.

'So many dams out here, the boys were taught as soon as they could walk,' Braden said when she'd commented.

189

Rory looked at her as though she'd suggested they walk to Augathella to the council pool. 'I don't think that's a very good idea.'

'What? What's wrong? Don't you want to swim?' Callie asked as she turned off the electronic whiteboard.

'Miss Callie,' Rory, always aloof, said politely. 'Look out the window.'

She walked across to the window at the other side of the room and stared.

And then frowned.

'What is it? Another dust storm?' The one she'd experienced in Mitchell a few weeks ago had been awful.

'No, it's a thunderstorm. When the sky goes that yukky yellow brown, it means we're gonna get thunder and lightning.'

'Going to, not gonna,' she corrected automatically as she stared at the eerie light outside.

'And lots of rain. Can the dogs and Bluey come inside?' Nigel asked screwing his face up.

'I'm scared of thunder,' Petie said holding onto her leg.

'How about we go in the middle of the house to the family room, and put a movie on, and we'll turn it up real loud so we can't hear the storm?'

Even as Callie spoke a loud clap of thunder shook the house.

'Quick, you guys go and choose a DVD and I'll bring the pups in. Then we'll have popcorn with the movie,' she said as three scared little faces looked up at her.

Quickly she ushered them down the hallway, and got the DVD going. When they were settled, she hurried to the door. 'Stay here, I won't be long.'

Another loud clap of thunder hit as she reached the back door. Two shivering pups and a determined red calf stared through the screen door, but there was no sign of Petie's pup, Cottie.

Opening the door a little, Callie pushed herself through so the calf couldn't get past her. Bluey had got in one afternoon last week and created havoc in the kitchen until they'd chased him up the hall and out the door into the breezeway. It had been wonderful to hear Nigel laugh as they'd all chased the calf.

She put her head down as a strong gust of dry hot wind preceded another clap of thunder. She'd never seen a storm like this before. The wind tore at her clothes as it swirled around her, gritty dust stinging her eyes and coating her lips. She bent down and picked up the two pups and carried them to the breezeway where she could shut the roller door, and lock them in. 'Come on, Bluey. You can go in there too.'

191

He followed as she knew he would. Any mess he made she'd clean up later. She got the two dogs and the calf in there safely, shut the roller door from the inside, and then went back through the screen door, into the house, down the hall and back out the kitchen door to look for Cottie.

The wind was even more ferocious now and as she looked to the west, a solid curtain of rain approached from the now-boiling clouds. As she scanned the yard looking for the missing pup, a cloud of dust swirled on the main drive into the property.

Thank goodness, it was Braden's ute.

'Cottie,' she yelled as she pushed against the wind. As she fought her way towards the dog enclosure a strong gust ripped a sheet of iron from the shed roof and lifted it into the air.

Callie screamed and ducked as the iron hit the ground only a metre in front of her. As she stopped, she spied movement behind the dog run. Cottie was cowering between the back fence and a tree. She put her head down to stop the dust getting in her eyes and hurried over to pick him up.

'Look out, Callie!' Braden's yell reached her over the howling wind.

***

Braden planted the accelerator when he saw Callie in the back yard. The wind was buffeting the ute, and debris was flying around the property. He jumped out of the ute and opened the main gate to the house yard. The storm was as bad as the one the night Julia had gone out in to rescue Taffee.

As he drove through the gate a sheet of iron lifted from the roof and speared into the backyard, barely missing Callie. Braden didn't stop to close the gate behind him. There'd be no cattle on the move in this storm.

What the hell was she doing outside? He thought she'd have more sense. All the memories of that dreadful afternoon two years ago came rushing back as the ute sped past the shed to the house.

'You're not going out in this storm, Julia,' he'd yelled. 'Don't be so bloody stupid.'

'Taffee's down at the dam. She'll be scared stiff.'

'I don't care. You're not going. It's a horse.'

'Stop me.' Her eyes had challenged him and he'd held her arm, aware of Rory and Nigel listening.

'No. I'll rely on your common sense. Taffee will be fine.'

'She'll be scared, Braden.'

'She'll be fine. Listen, I can hear Petie crying. You go and get him out of the cot, and I'll put the kettle on. I'll take you down in the ute when the wind eases.'

Rory and Nigel had followed him into the kitchen, and a couple of minutes later, Braden heard Petie crying again. At the same time, the sound of the quad bike reached him and Braden had raced to the back door in time to see Julia and the quad bike disappear into the teeming rain.

He would never forget that moment as long as he lived.

Gritting his teeth he flung the ute door open as another sheet of iron lifted from the side of the shed and twisted in the air towards Callie.

'Look out, Callie,' he yelled.

He watched in horror as the edge of the iron sliced down her arm and she pitched forward to the ground just as the rain hit.

Chapter 28

Callie heard the sheet of iron flex in the wind as it flew above her and from the corner of her eye she knew it was coming down. She dived to the left, and as the heavy sheet hit her left arm, she tripped over the pup who had come running to her.

Gathering the pup into her arms, she lay on her side with eyes closed, winded and fighting for breath, her arm stinging.

'Callie, oh God, Callie.' Braden kneeled beside her and he pulled both her and the pup into his arms. 'Please Callie, open your eyes. Look at me, sweetheart.'

As the rain lashed them, Braden's lips brushed her forehead and she opened her eyes and took a deep gasping breath.

'I'm all right. I'm just winded.' She looked up and the intensity of his gaze made her heart thunder in her chest.'

'I thought I'd lost you too.' His arms held her tightly, and no matter how much she wanted to, Callie resisted the urge to sink into his embrace.

She opened her mouth to speak, but before she could Braden's warm lips covered hers. Callie closed her eyes again, caught between heaven and

195

hell. This is what she'd dreamed of, but it wasn't right. She stiffened in his arms and the pup squirmed between them. But she couldn't resist and as she relaxed into his hold, her lips opened beneath his. The rain teemed down and finally Braden lifted his head away. His fingers were wet as he cupped her chin. 'We'd better go inside. Your arm's bleeding.'

She nodded mutely and sat up. The pup scampered off her chest towards the house.

'We need to talk about this later, Callie.' Braden's face was closed.

They made their way to the back door, and opened the door. A very wet pup left muddy footprints on the kitchen floor.

'Cottie,' Petie squealed and Callie's heart sank as she looked at the three boys at the window.

'Are you hurt, Miss Callie?' Rory's voice held concern.

'I'm fine, guys, thank you. Just a little scratch on my arm.'

'We saw the shed flying around the yard and we saw Daddy save you.' Nigel's smile was wide and Callie held back a groan. 'And he kissed you too.'

'Well,' she said brisky, without looking at Braden. 'I'm going to my place to have a shower and get some clean clothes on and then I have some popcorn to make.'

'And I'll put some betadine and a plaster on your arm. Is your tetanus vaccination up to date? And I'll walk you over.'

'Yes. It is, and I'm fine. I'd rather walk over myself, please.' Her heart was pounding and she needed some space. 'You need to be here with the boys.' Callie quickly opened the kitchen door and headed outside. Her thoughts were in such turmoil, she wasn't aware of the rain until she stepped into a huge puddle halfway to the donga.

Oh, shit, What the hell am I going to do?

She stood at the bottom of the steps and lifted her face to the rain, and the drops running down her face mingled with her tears.

***

Braden quickly changed out of his wet clothes, his heart thumping and his hands shaking.

'Bloody idiot,' he muttered under his breath, calling himself all kinds of a fool.

Why the hell did I do that?

Because he hadn't been able to stop himself. The relief when he had seen that Callie was not hurt had overwhelmed him and he'd lost the careful control he always kept in place. Although maybe not so careful if Kent had noticed him watching her last night.

197

'Who's a bloody idiot, Dad?'

His head flew up and his gaze settled on Nigel standing in the doorway.

'I am. I should have come home earlier before the storm hit. I should have made sure I was here to check that everyone was safe.'

'Miss Callie, looked after us, Dad.' Nigel's face screwed up in a frown. 'Will we still call her Miss Callie when she's our new mum, or will we call her Mummy?'

Braden froze as he pulled the dry T-shirt over his head. 'What?'

'She is going to be our new mum, isn't she? We need a new one, and Miss Callie is just right. You like her too because you kissed her.'

Braden swallowed and pulled his T-shirt down before he crouched in front of Nigel.

'Mate, Miss Callie is here to look after you, and to teach you. She is a lovely lady, and a good teacher and she is working very hard. She wants to keep you safe and happy, like I do, but we're not ready for a new mum yet.'

'But why not?' Nigel's bottom lip trembled and Braden reached out and pulled his son close as a surge of love hit him square in the chest. How could he have left his boys for so long? His selfish action as he'd wallowed in his grief had contributed to Nigel's unhappiness and it was up to him to dispel any hope of a new mum—yet—and not upset Nigel.

'Because we're just getting used to being us. You've only been back at home with me for a few weeks.' He smoothed back Nigel's hair and held his son's eyes with his as he searched for the right words.

'I do like Miss Callie very much, and we want to keep her here while she gets used to us. She's not used to the outback and cattle and puppies, so while she looks after us, we have to look after her too. While we do that I'm sure she'll be happy to stay and get used to us. Do you know what it means to try and make someone do something they don't want to do?'

'I do.' Nigel nodded slowly. 'I have to sit next to Amanda Brimble at school and I don't like that. I don't like her and she has a silly name.'

Braden's lips tugged in a smile. 'Okay. If we try to make Miss Callie do something she doesn't want, she'll feel the same way and she might want to go back to her house.'

Braden hoped his kiss hadn't done exactly that to her.

'So what do we do, Dad?'

'We all learn to live here together. We help Miss Callie and we don't say anything about new mums. What do you think about that?'

'I guess it's okay.'

'I love you, Nige, and your Mummy would be very proud of you too.'

'Why did she go away, Daddy?'

'It was a very sad accident, and it was her time to go.' Braden hated those platitudes; he'd heard the same phrases so many times at Julia's funeral and in the weeks afterward, but at six, Nigel wasn't old enough to hear of Braden's guilt.

'Can we have pizza now?'

Braden ruffled his son's hair. Strangely he felt calmer. Nigel had taken his thoughts away from his foolish behaviour. 'I think Miss Callie was going to make popcorn. Let's go see if she's back yet.'

Chapter 29

Callie left the big house before dinner and went back to her donga. She'd let Braden look at her arm, and held herself rigid while his warm fingers touched her bare skin.

'No need. It's just a minor cut,' she said. What she didn't tell him was that she was sure to be bruised as the iron had hit her hard, and her arm was aching.

'You were lucky. Just a nick that bled a little.' His voice held tension too; he was obviously embarrassed that he'd kissed her.

She wanted to cause the least fuss possible and just get out of there. Popping the corn had been tense; the silences in the kitchen had been long and heavy. A couple of times he had gone to speak, but she had shaken her head, and gone into the pantry, or up the hall to check on the boys.

'I'm not hungry. Are you right to get the boys something? There's some sausages thawed out in the fridge.'

'Yeah, sure,' he said. 'What about your dinner?'

'I'm not hungry,' she said again.

'Oh. Okay.' Braden's hand lifted towards her and then it dropped. 'Sleep well. And Callie?'

She froze and turned from the door. 'Yes?'

'We'll still do that drive tomorrow out to the river at the back of the property and take the boys for a picnic.'

She nodded and shut the door behind her.

No, *she* wouldn't be going on any picnic tomorrow. It was her day off and no man was telling her what to do. Anyway, Callie intended doing some very serious thinking tonight, and she wasn't even sure she would still be here tomorrow.

You promised Nigel, a little voice in her head interrupted.

Callie opened the door of her donga and sat down on the hard sofa. The room was quiet, the only sound was the whirring of her small refrigerator. No sounds of DVDs, little boys giggling or puppies playing. No sound of Braden telling the boys stories as they went to bed. No Silly Callie as Petie put his soft little hand in hers.

Leaning forward, Callie put her face in her hands. She should never have fled Brisbane and come here. Her arm throbbed painfully and her mind spun.

What should she do? Staying here would be awkward. Not because Braden had kissed her; she knew it was only a knee jerk reaction, his relief that she wasn't hurt. Pulling out her phone, she checked she had connection to the farm satellite and was pleased to see the connected icon.

She quickly dialled Jen's number, not even taking notice of what time it was.

'Cal, I'm so pleased you called. It's like you've dropped off the face off the planet.'

'Hi, Jen.'

'What's wrong. I can hear the tone of your voice. Are you okay?'

'Not really, I need some advice.'

'Fire away.' Jen's voice rose. 'Okay, I'll be five minutes. I'm on the phone. It's Callie.'

'Sorry, bad time?'

'Hon, every time is a bad time lately. The kids have been demanding. Damien is working lots of overtime and I'm going stir crazy.'

'Do you need a nanny?' Callie said quietly.

'Why? Are you offering? Hasn't it worked out?'

'Yes. No. Sort of?'

'What happened.'

'Braden kissed me.'

'The low life jerk. Where was his wife?'

'I didn't tell you the details, Jen. His wife died a couple of years ago and the three boys have been living with their aunty. It's just Braden and me and the three boys now. The boys are wonderful. And the problem is not really him. He's a really good guy.'

'I don't get it. He kissed you against your will, but he's a good guy.'

'Yes. I mean no. It wasn't against my will. It was unexpected.'

'Do you like him?'

'I do.'

'So what's the problem? Okay, I'm coming, Damien! Two minutes.'

'It's okay, Jen. You go.'

'No, he's fine. It's just that the kids are a bit of a handful at the moment and Damien's tired. Tell me what advice you want.'

'I don't know what to do. Should I stay or go?'

There was a long silence. 'I don't know what to tell you. I can only suggest one thing. Do what you feel is best for you. Okay? I'll call you tomorrow. Love you, Cal. And remember whatever happens we'll be here for you.'

Callie pressed end and stared at the phone.

What do I want?

I don't want to go through another Greg situation. I want to be happy.

Moving briskly, she went into the small bedroom at the back of the donga and pulled out her suitcase. A month ago she hadn't known this little family. Rory's and Nigel's and Petie's faces filled her mind, but she pushed them away. They were *not* her children. She was not family to them.

Opening the wardrobe, she pulled out her clothes and then cleared the bathroom cabinet with one sweep of her hand, and dropped it all into another small bag.

Insects chirped in the dark as Callie took one last look around the donga she had stayed in for the last month.

No regrets, she said to herself as a wave of nostalgia hit her in the chest. *Don't be stupid, it's a horrid donga.* Small, cramped and hot; think of your beautiful home on the river.

Strangely that didn't work.

Pulling the door closed quietly, she held the keys to Sophie's Camry wagon in her hand. She would leave it in town, and pick up her own car and drive back to Brisbane.

She would call Braden from wherever she was in the morning. She pulled a face; it would be Augathella because she wouldn't be able to get her car until eight a.m. She threw her one suitcase in the car. She'd sort out the jumpers and stuff that were still in the utility room cupboard down the track. She wouldn't need them at home anyway.

The Camry's engine purred to life and she drove slowly down the driveway keeping one eye on the main house, but there was no sign of life. As Callie got out and opened the gate, she felt like a thief in the night, but drew a deep breath and drove through and quickly got out and locked the gate behind her.

205

She hadn't driven in the dark on this road before, and she felt around the dashboard for the high beam switch. Eventually she found it, and then another switch below turned on the LED driving lights above the bumper bar, lighting up the road ahead.

Her thoughts swirled around and she took another deep breath.

Am I doing the right thing?

Am I leaving the boys—and Braden—in the lurch?

What was her problem anyway?

So Braden had kissed her. What was wrong with that?

Did you enjoy it?

Yes. I did.

Did your reaction frighten you?

Yes it did.

Why would that be, Calista Young?

Because I care about him. A lot. Too much. And those gorgeous boys.

Do you think this will hurt him?

As her conscience asked her that question, the bright lights of the Camry lit up the section of the road where she had first encountered Braden and the boys.

He had been so kind and thoughtful, and accepting of her. He'd fallen in the irrigation channel, and he'd retrieved her luggage. He was a good man. And she cared about him. A lot.

And what was she doing?

Running away like a coward.

Braden was not Greg.

Her foot hit the brake and she swung the steering wheel around so hard, for a moment she worried the car was going to roll.

But it settled on its four wheels and headed back down the road the way she had come.

A few minutes later she was through the gate, and had parked the Camry next to Braden's ute.

Chapter 30

Braden lifted his head and frowned as a car pulled up in the yard. He glanced up at the kitchen clock; it was heading for eight o'clock.

Kent?

He walked to the door and peered through the screen, surprised to see Sophie's Camry parked there. For a stupid moment, he forgot she was away and her car was garaged here now; he expected her to step out of the driver's side.

His frown deepened when Callie climbed out and he wondered why she was in the car.

God, she was leaving. Because he hadn't been able to control himself.

He held the screen door open as she walked quickly up the two steps.

Her cheeks were flushed and for a moment he worried that she was running a fever. Her eyes were bright as they held his.

'Where are the boys?'

'In the family room. I let them stay up because there's no school tomorrow. What's wrong?'

'I need to talk to you. Can we sit in the kitchen or out on the veranda?'

Braden's gut clenched. Callie *was* going to leave. She was here to say goodbye. He looked out at the car and the back veranda light lit up the interior. Sure enough her suitcase was on the back seat.

He lifted his hand and ran it through his hair.

'How about in the kitchen? I could do with a cuppa,' he said.

I could do with a strong drink.

Her eyes hadn't left him.

'Sit down and I'll make you a coffee.'

She nodded and did as he asked. As the jug boiled Braden crossed to the fridge and rummaged in the back.

'I hid these from the boys.' He held up a packet of Tim Tams.

'They must have been well hidden,' she said with a smile and his gut relaxed a bit.

'Behind the pumpkin.'

She smiled and Braden's hopes rose a little. If she was leaving she wouldn't look so damn relaxed . . . and beautiful.

Finally the jug boiled, the coffees were poured, and the biscuits were on the table.

Braden sat down and looked at Callie. Her eyes were still on his, but she was starting to look nervous.

He clenched his hands on the table. 'You're leaving, aren't you?'

'I was,' she said quietly. 'I got as far as the irrigation channel.'

'Then you remembered you'd signed a contract at the school.'

Her mouth opened to an O, and her eyes widened. 'Oh dear, I'd totally forgotten about that.'

'So, you said you *were* leaving?'

Callie nodded. 'I was. I got to where you rescued my luggage and I woke up to myself. You need me here,' she said simply.

'We do. And we want you here. There's a difference there, Callie.'

'I know there is.'

'I'm sorry I kissed you.'

'Are you?'

Her eyes were intent on his.

'I'm sorry I kissed you when I did. I'm not sorry I kissed you.' It was hard to look away from her, and his heart jumped when she smiled.

'I didn't mind you kissing me. I'm going to be honest, Braden. It's time for honesty. I came here because I was running away from a situation. I trusted a man and he let me down very publicly. I ran away.'

'I know. On a television broadcast.'

'You knew? You knew all the time?'

'Not all the time. Kent told me the other night. Jacinta told him. She recognised you.'

'Oh God, the school knows.' She put her hand over her eyes and then quickly dropped it away. 'But it doesn't matter, does it? It's not important.'

Braden reached over and took her hand and smiled when her fingers curled in his. 'Keep being honest with me, Callie. Why did you come back. Only because we need you?'

She shook her head and held his eyes. 'No. I came back because I care about the four of you. I couldn't leave. And I made a promise to Nigel. I can't let him down.'

He caressed the top of her hand with his thumb. 'It's been too fast and you've been thrown in at the deep end. With the work, the boys, and with me.'

'With you?'

'With the way I feel about you. I've got a suggestion. How about we start all over again, and get to know each other properly. Take our time. No rush. No expectations. Just so we both feel comfortable.'

'I think that's a good idea,' she said softly.

'So you'll stay?'

'Yes, I will.'

'Without rushing things and just this once, may I kiss you to show you how much I like that "yes"?'

Callie shook her head, and disappointment trickled into his heart. He'd blown it already.

'Sorr—' he began. But Callie stood and held one finger up. She came around to his side of the table and put her hands on each side of his face.

'No, I'll kiss you to show you I mean it.'

She stood beside him and he lifted his face to meet her lips. As her soft sweet lips met his, footsteps thundered down the hall and Rory came bursting into the kitchen, holding Braden's phone.

'Dad! It's Aunty Sophie and she really needs to talk to you.' He shoved the phone into Braden's hand.

Braden lifted his other hand and reached for Callie. She squeezed his fingers.

'Stay where you are, Miss Callie. We'll finish this later.'

'Dad!' Rory was hopping from foot to foot. 'Talk to Aunty Sophie. She's crying really bad. Quick, Dad!'

Braden frowned and took the phone, lifting it to his ear. 'Soph? It's me. Are you okay?'

A long shuddering sob drowned out Rory's incessant talking. 'No.'

'Sophie?'

'Bray? Can I come home please. To stay? I want to come home. I have to come home.' Braden's gaze met Callie's as his little sister sobbed into the phone.

'Of course you can come home, Soph. Do you want me to come and get you?'

Callie reached out and held his hand. 'Whatever you need me to do, I can help,' she said.

'Thank you,' he said, pulling her close as he continued to listen to Sophie.

UNTIL THE NEXT STORY...

Callie and Sophie's stories continue in *Outback Sky* when we meet two new arrivals to *Kilcoy Station.*

Fallon Malone is a loner, refusing to rely on anyone else for her happiness. She's content being her own boss, working in the skies of the remote Queensland outback. When she begins her contract in the Augathella region for the annual cattle muster, Fallon is unimpressed with the new station manager.

Jon Ogilvie is equally unhappy with this new female bush pilot, hired by Kent Mason, owner of neighbouring *Lara Waters*. Now that Braden has his kids back, he seems to have lost his focus on best practice for the local cattle stations. It also doesn't help that Fallon Malone is a law unto herself.

As the stockman and bush pilot come head-to-head, nature conspires to bring them together. Can Fallon and Jon overcome their differences and give in to the attraction that refuses to go away?

The Augathella Girls series.

Book 1: Outback Roads -The Nanny

Book 2: Outback Sky -The Pilot

Book 3: Outback Escape – The Sister

Book 4: Outback Winds – The Jillaroo

Book 5: Outback Dawn – The Visitor

Book 6: Outback Moonlight – The Rogue

Book 7: Outback Dust – The Drifter

Book 8: Outback Hope – The Farmer

Visit Annie's website to subscribe to her newsletter to stay up to date with release dates:

OTHER BOOKS from ANNIE

Whitsunday Dawn
Undara
Osprey Reef
East of Alice (2022)

Porter Sisters Series

Kakadu Sunset

Daintree

Diamond Sky

Hidden Valley

Larapinta

Pentecost Island Series

Pippa

Eliza

Nell

Tamsin

Evie

Cherry

Odessa

Sienna

Tess

Isla

The Augathella Girls Series (2022)

Outback Roads (February)

Outback Skies (April)

Outback Escape (June)

Plus more to follow

Sunshine Coast Series

Waiting for Ana

The Trouble with Jack

Healing His Heart

Sunshine Coast Boxed Set

The Richards Brothers Series

The Trouble with Paradise

Marry in Haste

Outback Sunrise

Bondi Beach Love Series

Beach House

Beach Music

Beach Walk

Beach Dreams

The House on the Hill

Second Chance Bay Series

Her Outback Playboy

Her Outback Protector

Her Outback Haven

Her Outback Paradise

The McDougalls of Second Chance Bay Boxed Set

Love Across Time Series

Come Back to Me

Follow Me

Finding Home

The Threads that Bind

Others

Deadly Secrets

Adventures in Time

Silver Valley Witch

The Emerald Necklace

Worth the Wait

Ten Days in Paradise

Her Christmas Star

An Aussie Christmas Duo

About the Author

Annie lives in Australia, on the beautiful north coast of New South Wales. She sits in her writing chair and looks out over the tranquil Pacific Ocean. She writes contemporary romance and loves telling the stories that always have a happily ever after. She lives with her very own hero of many years and they share their home with Toby, the naughtiest dog in the universe, and Barney, the rag doll puss, who hides when the four grandchildren come to visit.

Stay up to date with her latest releases at her website: **http://www.annieseaton.net**

If you would like to stay up to date with Annie's releases, subscribe to her newsletter here: http://www.annieseaton.net

Made in United States
Troutdale, OR
01/28/2024

17250803R00137